GW00984110

A message from the author...

Thank you so much for buying a copy of this book, it really makes me smile that children (and grown-ups) are reading and enjoying my stories.

By purchasing this book, not only are you making me do a little happy dance, but you are also supporting The Play Well Trust, my non-profit organisation, which uses the power of play to support children who are seriously ill and their families. I donate 20% of profits from all sales of my books to The Play Well Trust, which enables us to support more children and families through play based activities.

To find out more about the work we do at The Play Well Trust, visit our website: www.theplaywelltrust.com or find us on Facebook, Instagram and Twitter!

And, as a big thank you, here is the link to my other website, The Do Try This at Home School, where you will find a wide range of **FREE**, creative learning activities that you can try at home as a family. Lots of fun for everyone!

www.thedotrythisathomeschool.com

Again, you can also find us on Facebook, Instagram and Twitter.

I hope you enjoy the story, my other books are also available on Amazon and all links are on my websites.

Thank you for your support,

Sarah Vaughan

For Bryn, who inspires me every day...

Chapter One

Timmy Turner was a stick of a boy with scruffy brown hair and eyes like chocolate buttons. He lived in a small terraced house on a long street with his parents – Mr and Mrs Turner – his little brother and sister – Peter and Rosie – and a sausage dog called Mr Poops.

Timmy was a happy little boy and he was especially happy when he was daydreaming about amazing inventions he wanted to make with his dad in their rickety old shed at the end of the garden. Timmy's dad was a fantastic inventor and they would spend hours in the shed together at weekends building their ideas.

Once, they made a World War One aeroplane, The Red Baron. It was so big that Timmy could actually sit inside and, secretly (between you and me), he was working on an engine to make it fly.

Timmy was a very clever boy who loved science, history and inventing things. His teacher, however, thought he was stupid. A daydreamer who would never amount to anything.

Miss Hardvile was as nasty as her name suggests. She was a hard, vile, wicked old woman with bony elbows, a crooked nose and a whiskery chin. Her teeth were the colour of a good mature cheddar cheese and Timmy thought that she had probably started teaching around the time of the dinosaurs.

She delighted in making the children in her class miserable with daily times-table tests and hours of boring homework.

Harriet Hardvile, as far as Timmy could tell, was the sort of person who was never happy, and I mean never. If the fluffiest unicorn in the world had skipped up to her with a diamond tiara and a bunch of balloons filled with happiness, she would have popped every balloon on the unicorn's rainbow horn and poked the tiara up his nose.

Timmy believed that this miserable persona was the very reason that Miss Hardvile had remained a 'Miss' all her life.

After all, nobody could marry such a hard and vile person, could they?

However, there was a side to Harriet Hardvile that nobody ever saw at school. There was one thing that raised a smile on that wicked old face and melted that frozen exterior, and that was Frou-Frou.

Frou-Frou was Miss Hardvile's best friend. A tiny little, shoe-wearing Chihuahua that she utterly adored. Her house was full of photographs of little Frou-Frou dressed up in a whole variety of doggy outfits, from scuba-diving Frou-Frou to Frou-Frou in a tutu. There were tiny doggy shoes and hats, going out outfits, staying in outfits and outfits for popping out to the garden, complete with umbrella hat, just in case it rained.

This tiny little canine had her very own master bedroom in Harriet Hardvile's house, where she slept on antique eiderdowns on a super-king-size bed. Harriet herself slept in a single bed in the tiny box room next door.

Every year on Frou-Frou's birthday, Harriet Hardvile would throw an extravagant party for all Frou-Frou's doggy friends. There would be balloons, performance artistes, a photo booth for yet more dressing up, doggy champagne (which was water in plastic champagne flutes) and, of course, the biggest doggy birthday cake you have ever seen. It was so big that little Frou-Frou could have quite happily lived inside it.

All of the dog walkers from the park thought two things about Miss Hardvile:

1. That she was a kind and caring person.
2. That she was barking mad!

They all came to the parties every year because they too were barking mad, and also the party bags that were given out at the end were full of very expensive doggy treats for Frou-Frou's little friends.

Frou-Frou was Harriet Hardvile's one and only source of happiness. As soon as she was away from her little friend, she turned into the meanest, cruellest person you'd ever hope not to meet.

So how, and most importantly why, did this woman end up in the world of teaching? She had never wanted to be a teacher. When she was a little girl, she dreamed of being a zookeeper or a fashion designer, but the Hardvile family had other ideas.

You see, Harriet Hardvile was descended from a long line of teachers. Her parents were teachers, her parents' parents were teachers and even her parents' parents' parents were teachers. If you yourself have ever had a good teacher, you will know that this equals a lot of teachers!

Miss Hardvile, an only child, did exactly what her parents expected of her. She studied hard, learned facts, trained to be a teacher and then got a job at Timmy's school, where she had remained, terrorising small children, for decades. She very much resented that fact and every day it made her a little more bitter and twisted. As a result, being a small child in her class was a terrifying experience to say the least.

Luckily, Timmy had some very good friends at school and every playtime they would think of wild and imaginative ways to scare Miss Hardvile from the classroom, never to return again. These ideas ranged from stink bombs in her handbag to slime in her coffee mug and even a rocket that would attach to the back of her chair and send her flying around the classroom, out of the window and off into space, but, sadly, they had not been brave enough to put any of their plans into action... yet.

******

The best thing about school, Timmy thought, was the school holidays. And one particular half term, Timmy was lying on his bed enjoying one of his favourite books, which was called "The Amazing History of Everything". He was also enjoying a large glass of Mr Busy's Fizzy Whizzy Pop. This was his favourite drink, mainly because it made him do enormous BURPS that shook the room! Mrs Turner did not let him have it very often, but, as he was on school holidays, he was allowed a treat.

The other side effect of Mr Busy's Fizzy Whizzy Pop was that it made Timmy wee... A LOT! Timmy had reached an especially exciting part of his book all about the Ancient Egyptians, and how the peasants building the pyramids managed to move the enormous stones without being squashed as flat as a pancake. But it was no good, he had to stop reading, as the fizzy pop was having its usual effect. He was going to have to make a run for the toilet.

Jumping off his bed, Timmy made a dash for the door. His journey to the bathroom would not be an easy one: first, he would need to tiptoe between Peter's train tracks, which he was playing with on the landing, and then scramble into the bathroom without standing on the tiny hairbrushes that were strewn across the floor where Rosie had been playing pony hairdressers. One false move could end in a painful injury.

One last jump over Mr Poops, who was fast asleep outside the bathroom door, and Timmy finally made it to the toilet – just in time. Phew!

When he had finished, he flushed the toilet and washed his hands (properly, with the soap between his fingers, front and back, just like his mum had told him to. She would often sing "If you don't wash your hands when you go to the loo, you might get a tummy ache and have runny….")

Well, you get the idea!

As Timmy washed his hands and hummed his song, he looked at the water swirling around the plughole. He noticed it was all going in a clockwise direction. Looking into the flushing toilet, he saw that exactly the same thing was happening.

Now most children would think 'Hmmm, that's nice,' and go on their merry way, but not Timmy. Oh no! Timmy was a curious child and he wanted to know why. Why did the water flow clockwise? What if it went the other way, like it does on the other side of the world? Would it change the space–time continuum? (Probably not but, hey, it was worth a try.)

Timmy set about filling the sink and pulling the plug. He tried everything he could to make the water flow the other way and used all the tools he had to hand – toothbrushes, dad's shaving foam, Rosie's pony hairbrushes and a little yellow rubber duck – but nothing would change the direction of the swirling water.

Maybe the toilet would be different, he thought, but for flush after flush the same thing happened. Then an idea hit him like a bolt of lightning. When I pull the lever down, the water flows this way, he thought, so, therefore, when I push the lever upwards it MUST flow the other way. (Don't try this at home, kids!)

Like any good scientist, Timmy pondered his theory some more. It made perfect sense and he concluded that he should test his hypothesis. Stepping up to the toilet, he reached out his hand, grabbed the lever and gently pushed it upwards while looking at the water below him.

At first nothing happened, so he did it again. Still nothing. He was about to give up, but then Timmy noticed that the water *was* starting to move in the opposite direction. Woooo! He was right! But what happened next, Timmy could never have predicted.

Right before his eyes, the water in the toilet started to change colour. At first, it was green and a bit whiffy! Timmy wondered if this was the effect of Mr Busy's Fizzy Whizzy Pop in the plumbing, but then the spinning water started to fill with all sorts of colours: pink, brown, electric blue, violet and orange! Round and round it went. Timmy could feel himself getting dizzy. Suddenly, there was a huge blue flash that made Timmy shut his eyes. Mr Poops came running into the bathroom to see what was happening.

There was a loud POP and a BANG and, as quick as a flush, Timmy and Mr Poops were gone!

Chapter Two

Opening his eyes, Timmy noticed at once that he was surrounded by swirling, colourful water and flashing lights. "I don't know who installed our plumbing," he yelled to Mr Poops, "but I don't think they were qualified."

Faster and faster they hurtled through the water, around twists and bends, upside down, round and round. They even did a loop-the-loop. It was like being on a psychedelic water slide. "We'll call this phenomenon 'The Super Duper Pooper Slide'. This is BRILLIAAAAAANT!" shrieked Timmy. He was having the time of his life. Mr Poops had covered his eyes with his long furry ears and was humming a little doggy song to himself. He wanted to get off this ride *at once*.

Suddenly, there was an almighty crash and the pair came to an abrupt halt. The water disappeared and the colours faded into darkness.

As Timmy's senses gradually returned to him, he realised that they were no longer in his little terraced house in England. Now they were in a hot, dark room. A hot, dark, smelly room. Poor Mr Poops had clearly noted the pungent pong emanating from this place. His face was a picture of utter disgust! Timmy slowly stood up and tried to find his bearings, when a deep voice came from out of the darkness.

"Pass me a leaf, boy," it demanded.

"I beg your pardon?" Timmy replied.

"Pass me a leaf," said the voice with more urgency.

"What on earth for?"

"You know, to wipe my rear end. I've just done my business and now I need to wipe and I've run out of leaves in my basket."

'Well, that explains the smell,' thought Mr Poops.

Timmy was just about to ask what sort of business the voice was in, when suddenly it dawned on him exactly where he was. He was still in a bathroom, but it wasn't like his modern DIY-store bargain suite, it was a bathroom he'd been reading about earlier in his history book. Looking behind him, he saw that his own toilet was now also in the room, hidden away in a shadowy corner.

"COME ON, BOY! I haven't got all day. I've got to get back to work."

Timmy quickly grabbed a leaf from a basket at the side of the room, passed it to the outstretched hand and headed swiftly for the door.

Stepping into the bright light and sweltering heat, Timmy took a big breath of fresh air and his suspicions were confirmed. "We're in Ancient Egypt, Mr Poops! This is A-mazing!"

Timmy and Mr Poops were standing in the middle of a very busy and extremely noisy market. There were people selling all sorts of things and Timmy listened to their cries.

"Onions! Get your onions here. Full of oniony goodness they are!"

"Fresh bread! Get your fresh bread here. It's a bit rough around the edges... and the middle, but it's great for digestion."

"Behold, our latest invention. Sweets! They are delicious... and much nicer than his onions."

"Oi!" yelled the onion seller.

Timmy and Mr Poops wandered through the market, taking in the sights and smells and watching the people go about their daily business. He was even able to barter with a street seller to get himself a piece of cloth, using a few pennies that he had found in his pocket. He tore it in two and tied half of it around his head like a bandana to ease the heat of the blazing sun, and he used the other half to make a little sun cape for Mr Poops. The pair looked like they were going to a fancy-dress party, but Timmy didn't care. It wasn't like he was going to meet anyone who knew him in Ancient Egypt.

At the end of one line of stalls, they came to an opening and, looking up, Timmy saw the most spectacular sight. There in front of him, across a small stretch of desert, were a group of enormous pyramids.

"Wow!" gasped Timmy, gazing up at the epic, sparkling structures. They were so new and shiny that they glistened in the blazing sun. "That really is a wonder," he said to Mr Poops. They stood for some time taking in the spectacular scene. Suddenly, a large hand gripped Timmy's shoulder, making him jump out of his skin.

"Beautiful, aren't they?" Timmy recognised the gruff voice immediately as the voice from the toilet. He hoped the owner of the voice had washed his hands properly!

"I built them," said the man, "with my own fair hands... And a bit of help from the peasants who live around here."

Turning round, Timmy finally saw the owner of the voice. He was a huge man, almost a giant, with short, dark hair and arms as big as tree trunks. He was wearing a white tunic with a piece of rope around the waist and some brown sandals. 'He looks just like one of the men from my book,' Timmy thought.

"They are beautiful pyramids," Timmy said to the man. "How on earth did you manage to build them so perfectly?"

"Well, when you are a master craftsman, like me, it just comes naturally."

"I'm sure it does," said Timmy. "But how did you get those enormous stones up the sides of the pyramid?"

"With my own bare hands," said the man, proudly flexing his enormous biceps.

Timmy could quite believe that this giant of a man had lifted those blocks, with a little help from a few hundred peasants.

"They call me Seth," the man went on. "It means 'god of the storms and the desert'. I used my powerful storm-like forces to build this pyramid in the desert. We lost a few weaklings along the way. There were a couple of squashings, which made a terrible mess, but we did it!"

"That is truly amazing," said Timmy, in awe of such a Herculean human. "I'm Timmy Turner. It means 'misunderstood daydreamer'." Timmy had made that last bit up, but he felt that it was a good description of himself, "And this is Mr Poops," he went on. He decided that Mr Poops' name was probably self-explanatory.

Seth looked down at Timmy and Mr Poops, "Good to meet you young man. You clearly have a good eye for building prowess. I'm building another pyramid around the back, if you want to have a look. With those skinny arms, you won't be much use to me, but you are welcome to come and meet the builders."

"Really?" smiled Timmy. "That would be fantastic!"

Timmy and Mr Poops followed Seth across the desert, over to the glittering pyramid. It was even more beautiful up close.

"We're building these for the Pharaoh," said Seth. "For when he pops his clogs and heads off to the afterlife. He needs somewhere to keep all of his treasure, and his servants, and food... and him. So he asked me to put up a pyramid or two."

"Impressive," said Timmy.

"Yeah. Only he doesn't like these ones now. He wants a bigger one, a bit closer to the Nile."

"But nowhere is close to the River Nile here. This is a desert."

"Ah, young man, you underestimate us. If the pyramids won't come to the river, then the river will come to the pyramids."

Seth waved a giant hand towards what Timmy now realised was a long waterway. It was busy with boats and people unloading the enormous glistening rocks, using logs as rollers, winches on wooden structures and a lot of brute strength.

There were thousands of men swarming around the pyramid base, all wearing grubby white cloth outfits that were wrapped around them in various forms, and all of them were extremely busy. Timmy thought they looked a lot like worker ants in an ant colony. Each man clearly had a job to do, whether it was cutting stone blocks, mixing cement, unloading boats or building platforms to climb the sides of the mighty pyramid, and, come what may, every man was going to do his job.

As they got closer, it was clear that Seth was the equivalent to the queen ant. Every man who noticed him coming picked up his pace immediately. Timmy wondered how on earth these men could work at all in the sweltering heat.

Reaching the pyramid base, two large men came to greet Seth. They looked almost as gigantic as the boss himself and Timmy couldn't help but notice a family resemblance.

"These are my brothers," said Seth. "They keep an eye on things when I'm off-site. Boys, this is Timmy Turner. He's a... a... what *is* your job, young man?"

Timmy had to think quickly. What on earth did young boys do for work in Ancient Egypt? He knew that very few children got an education in a school and that most children were taught at home – they were taught to be helpful within whatever line of work the family was in.

"I'm just a farm hand," Timmy said. "I help my father on the farm where he works, but I'd love to be a builder of great monuments, just like you."

He looked to the men for a response. His flattery seemed to have got him somewhere, because three giant faces were smiling down at him. He could see rows of broken, greyish teeth in their enormous bearded mouths.

"Well, as I said, you might need to get some bigger muscles before you start working for us," laughed Seth, holding up Timmy's skinny arm. "But eat well and you never know! Now, let me introduce my brothers. This is Kha," he said, pointing at one of the men, "and this is Irsu."

"It's good to meet you," smiled Timmy, absentmindedly holding out his hand to shake theirs, and instantly regretting that decision. They almost turned his tiny hand to dust with their grip.

"How's it going, boys?" Seth asked his brothers.

"Well, my men are working hard," replied Kha, "unloading the boats and moving the blocks to the base."

"And my men are working hard adding the blocks to the pyramid," said Irsu. "But really, Seth, the trouble is they are just not working hard enough. They keep complaining of hunger and thirst and exhaustion, you know – like I care or something. If we're not careful, Anubis will have taken the Pharaoh to the afterlife before we've had a chance to finish."

"Hmmmm, maybe we should increase their hours and have them work through the night as well," pondered Seth aloud.

"Good idea," agreed Kha. "That would double our man hours if we work them night and day."

"What do you think, Timmy Turner?" asked Seth. "If you were in charge, how would you get the men to work harder so we can get this pyramid finished?"

Timmy had been watching the poor workers slaving away in the hot sun, lifting the enormous boulders off the boats, moving them to the pyramid on giant log rollers and hoisting them into place using winches and sheer man power. He was amazed by these workers.

"Well," said Timmy bravely, "I would follow the advice that you have just given me. I would give them a break, where I would encourage them to eat and drink well and to build their muscles, so that they can be of more use to you when they are working."

He looked up at the three giants, who wouldn't have looked out of place in The World's Strongest Man Competition, and suddenly he felt completely terrified. He knew that this was not the kind of response that these macho men were looking for.

For a second, three angry faces bore down on Timmy. He held his breath and Mr Poops covered his eyes with his paws. Then, the three brothers burst into fits of laughter. They laughed and laughed, holding their giant bellies until tears rolled down their cheeks.

"A BREAK!" Seth roared hysterically. "The men aren't working hard enough, so we should make them work less? That's the funniest thing I've ever heard! Don't give up your day job, Timmy Farm-Hand Turner." All three brothers were now doubled over with laughter.

Timmy's initial terror now turned to anger. In fact, the more they laughed at him, the angrier he became.

"ACTUALLY," snapped Timmy, over the giggles of the sniggering giants, "it's a proven fact, where I come from, that small breaks make for much more productive workers."

"And where do you come from?" laughed Kha. "It had better not be Rome! I can't stand those Romans with their gladiators and fancy sandals. They are so la dee da!"

"No!" cried Timmy. "I'm not from Rome. I come from a place you will never know of. A place where children are educated and houses have indoor plumbing."

This tipped the three giants over the edge. They were rolling around on the floor in utter hysterics.

"Educating children!" wailed Irsu. "What a waste of time!"

"And indoor plumbing!" added Seth. "Whoever heard of such a disgusting idea... except the Romans!" More hysterical laughter ensued.

"I bet I can improve productivity by tomorrow afternoon," yelled a now-furious Timmy Turner, before he'd really thought about the words that were tumbling from his mouth.

Suddenly, the men stopped laughing. They stood up and Seth looked Timmy squarely in the eye.

"I'm a betting man," he said menacingly. Timmy shuffled his feet in the sand, deeply regretting his outburst. "Let's see..." Seth went on. "If you win our bet, I will make you an honorary member of the Pyramid Builders' Association. However, if you lose, I will take that little pooch of yours and turn him into a nice handbag for the missus."

Poor Mr Poops looked pale, and that's not easy for a sausage dog!

Timmy hoped very much that Seth was joking about his second comment, although he thought that perhaps he wasn't. Now he'd got himself into this mess, there was only one way out, and that was to prove that he was right. He put his hand out to shake Seth's.

"Deal," he said in a determined tone, although inside he felt wobblier than his gran's raspberry jelly.

"You'd better get to work then, young man. These workers are dropping like flies. They keep complaining about being thirsty or something."

The enormity of the task ahead suddenly hit Timmy like a large stone falling from a pyramid, but he was not going to let it show.

"Right," he said, "where can I get supplies?"

"What do you need?" asked Seth.

"I need: some sort of fabric for making a roof, some fresh water, fruit and maybe some bread. Do you have tea here?"

"What's tea?"

"It's a hot drink we have at home."

"A hot drink, in a hot desert? No! We have beer and everyone drinks it, except our animals – they are allowed water from the Nile."

"Well, then beer will have to do," said Timmy, trying to sound manly.

"I'll tell you what I'll do," Seth continued, "seeing as you are such a bony little runt, and I like your determination and guts: I'll lend you my brother Kha to help you out. He's known in these parts as the Geezer of Giza. You tell him what you want and he'll get it for you, no questions asked."

Kha cracked his knuckles. Timmy gulped.

"Thank you," said Timmy hesitantly. "That's... erm, really helpful."

Although he was a little apprehensive, he was also relieved to have someone to help him with his monumental challenge.

"Come on then boys," boomed Seth. "Back to work. I've got a bet to win!" And he strode off confidently towards the construction site with Irsu.

Timmy looked up at Kha. He was indeed a giant of a man, just like his brothers, but, despite this, he seemed to be waiting for his instructions like a puppy waiting for someone to throw a ball. Timmy took the opportunity to take control.

"To the market!" he commanded, and he began to walk purposefully back towards the market stalls with Kha and

Mr Poops following close behind.

Chapter Three

Back in the hustle and bustle of the market, Timmy set about finding stalls that sold everything he needed. The first thing he would need was a basket to carry it all back to his makeshift café. He turned to Kha. "We need a lot of supplies," he said. "Do you think you could carry two baskets? I can only carry one."

Kha smiled. Timmy could see bits of food stuck to his giant broken teeth. "Don't waste time with baskets boy. What we need is a cart."

"But I don't have any money for a cart."

"We don't need money lad. We work for the Pharaoh."

Kha clapped his enormous hands together twice. It sounded like thunder. Suddenly, a crowd of people assembled in front of him. Timmy was amazed.

"Good afternoon everyone," bellowed Kha. "I am here with this young man, on a mission for the Pharaoh. We require many supplies for the builders of the Great Pyramids, and we need them now. The first thing we need is an ox and cart, as our goods will be heavy."

"No problem," came a shout from a man in the crowd, "I'll get mine." And he disappeared off into the market. Timmy stood in silence, staring at this giant commander. Kha beckoned him over.

"Timmy here will tell you what else we need."

Timmy looked at the group of people in front of him. He didn't like public speaking and his mouth was as dry as an Ancient Egyptian's sandy sandal. But then he remembered his bet with Seth and the potential fate of Mr Poops, and he pulled himself together, cleared his throat and said: "We need a large piece of fabric and some wooden poles and string to build a large shade for the workers."

"I'll get that," came another voice from the crowd.

"We also need beer, cups, bread, fruit and any other food that will give our workers extra energy. Some water for the animals and maybe a sausage for my dog."

The crowd dispersed and Timmy and Kha sat in the shade of a leafy fig tree to await their shopping order. 'No wonder Mum always gets her shopping delivered,' thought Timmy. This was much easier than getting everything yourself.

His thoughts were interrupted as a large, plump fig fell from the tree and landed next to him. He picked it up and looked suspiciously at the fruit.

"Have you never seen a fig before?" asked Kha.

"No," said Timmy. "We only have grapes and oranges where I come from. I've never eaten a fig."

"Grapes?" questioned Kha. "Are you sure you're not a Roman?"

"NO! I'm not!"

"Well, you should try a fig. They are delicious, and you must be hungry."

Now Timmy thought about it, yes, he was hungry, but he had no idea how to eat a fig. He looked at Kha for some sort of assistance. Kha stood up, picked a purple fruit from the tree and said, "The best way to eat a fig is inside out and upside down."

"Inside out?" quizzed Timmy. "And upside down? How on earth do you do that?"

Kha turned his fig upside down. He pinched the base and ripped the fruit open. Inside, Timmy could see juicy, cream-coloured flesh packed with bright orange seeds. It did look tasty.

He copied Kha, turning his fig upside down and pinching the base before ripping it open. Kha made this task look much easier in his giant hands than it really was, but Timmy managed eventually.

"Right," said Kha, "then you tear it in half, fold it inside out and eat." He shoved half of his fig into his mouth. "It stops you getting sore lips," he mumbled with his mouth full.

Timmy did as he was instructed and pushed the fig into his mouth. It was heavenly, with a sweet, honey-like taste. He quickly finished the first half and ate the other.

"You go steady with that, my boy," laughed Kha. "You'll be running to the toilet if you eat too many too fast!"

"Oh!" said Timmy, remembering the rather unpleasant experience of his arrival. "Thanks for the tip." He chewed more slowly and savoured the taste.

Mr Poops had been given a sausage and some water from one of the market traders. He had clearly enjoyed this and was now relaxing in the shade next to Timmy. This was the most surreal experience of their lives, Timmy thought. One minute they were at home, playing in the bathroom, running taps and flushing the toilet, and the next they had been sucked through the plumbing of time itself and now they were sitting in Ancient Egypt, under a fig tree, with a giant pyramid builder named Kha. It was certainly not an average sort of school-holiday day, but Timmy thought it was probably the best day ever.

Before too long a large cart appeared, laden with all of their shopping and pulled by a handsome-looking ox.

"Wow!" said Timmy. "You really have got everything we needed and even more than we asked for."

"Well, they don't call me the Geezer of Giza for nothing!" smiled Kha.

"Indeed!" giggled Timmy.

"Thank you everyone," waved Kha, to no one in particular, "Seth will make sure that you are paid for all of your hard work and generosity." He turned to Timmy. "Right then Timmy Turner, you'd better put your money where your mouth is and see if you can win this bet."

"Absolutely!" he replied enthusiastically.

They trudged back across the scorching desert, leading the huge brown ox and cart full of supplies, and headed towards the pyramid construction site.

****

Once back at the pyramids, Timmy found a shady spot

beneath a group of palm trees. "This should be perfect," he

said.

The ox sheltered beneath the trees with a well-deserved

wooden bucket of water.

"First things first, we need to build a shelter for when the

sun is at its highest. Where would you suggest, Kha?"

Kha looked around, held his thumb up in the air like some

sort of imaginary ancient compass, spun around and said,

"I'd put it right here, Timmy. That will keep you out of the sun and give you lots of shade for the workers to rest in."

"Perfect," said Timmy. "We need to unload the poles, twine and cloth from the cart."

"I'll get you a couple of helpers," replied Kha. "Otherwise we'll be here all day."

"Good thinking. We make quite the team, don't we?"

Kha smiled. Within no time at all, a group of six workers had constructed a large rectangular shelter using the poles, twine and cloth. They also brought some old scaffold planks and constructed a counter where Timmy could serve the food, and a large table and benches for the workers to sit at. These builders were phenomenal and, although the café was a little rustic to look at, Timmy felt that it had a certain charm about it.

He found some charcoal from an old fire and drew his own hieroglyphics on the front of his counter – these consisted of a stick man, a cup, a loaf of bread and a smiley face. He felt sure that people would understand his language.

When the work was complete, Timmy thought that he should reward these amazing workers by inviting them to be the first to have some food and drink in his new café. So, while they were tidying up, Timmy busied himself with unloading the cart, putting everything away and preparing a small meal for the workers. He set the table, poured each of the workers a beer from a barrel that had been donated to him and tore up some bread for them.

The workers were astonished: they were going to be allowed to have food and a break at work! They had never seen anything like this before and they were all very grateful for the opportunity. They ate and drank like they hadn't had anything in days. Timmy suspected that, for some of them, this may well have been the case.

When they had finished, one of the workers stood up and said, "Timmy Turner, you have fed us, watered us and allowed us to rest. Now I feel like I can work ten times as hard. Three cheers for Timmy!"

The other men joined in with the hip hip hoorays!

"I'm glad to have been of service," smiled Timmy. "Now, please do work ten times as hard, as Mr Poops' life depends on you."

Mr Poops, who had been remarkably helpful by sleeping behind the counter, sauntered out and did his very best puppy eyes.

"Ahhhhhh!" sighed all the builders, including Kha.

Then, remembering who he was, Kha said, "Right, boys, you heard the lad. Thank you for all your help, now please crack on and get this pyramid finished!"

"Yes sir!" chorused the workers, and off they went.

Kha, impressed by what he had seen, spent the rest of the day selecting groups of workers and sending them to Timmy's café for a break.

Timmy spent the rest of the day serving food and drink and washing up in some rickety old buckets filled with water from the Nile. He was so busy that he had to send the ox and cart back to the market with a worker to bring more supplies. Men rested in the shade and Timmy could see a difference in them by the time they left. He hoped beyond hope that this would be enough to increase their productivity and help him win the bet. After all, he was doing this to save the life of Mr Poops.

Mr Poops, who was somewhat oblivious to his impending doom, spent the rest of the day entertaining the workers, practising his puppy eyes and lying on his back to have his tummy tickled. Everyone loved Mr Poops.

As the sun began to sink below the horizon, the café became quiet and Timmy finally had a chance to look towards the pyramid. He could see that a lot of progress had been made – almost a whole line of stones had been placed along one of the sides. But was this more or less than usual?

Three silhouettes appeared in the heat haze. For a minute, Timmy wondered if it was a mirage, but then he realised that it was Seth, Irsu and Kha. They were walking towards his café like three mythical giants. Once again, Timmy felt sick to his stomach. He picked up Mr Poops and held him tight.

"I won't let them hurt you, my friend," he whispered.

Timmy tried to make out the looks on their faces, but it wasn't easy. The light was fading. Before long, all three men had reached the café and sat down at the table. Seth banged his fist on the table and shouted "BEER!" Timmy quickly poured each brother a beer, took them to the table and then retreated behind the counter.

The brothers were looking at bits of papyrus, frowning, then smiling, then counting on their fingers and then mumbling amongst themselves.

Timmy was terrified. What if he was wrong and Seth was right all along? Why did he ever think he could win a bet with Seth? After all, he wasn't a Master Pyramid Builder, he was a school boy. Suddenly, the words of his teacher, Miss Hardvile, filled his head. "You are a stupid boy, Timmy Turner, and you will never amount to anything. Why are you STILL using your fingers to count? You are too old for that. Why don't you grow up?"

Timmy swallowed back his tears in a big gulp.

"TIMMY!" roared Seth. "Pour yourself a beer and come and sit down." Timmy didn't dare argue. He did exactly as he was told and sat at the table to await his fate.

For a few seconds there was absolute silence. Timmy sat in front of the three brothers like a contestant on one of those reality TV shows. He felt sick to his stomach and took a large gulp of beer in the hope it would boost his courage. It tasted utterly disgusting, but it did make Timmy's head feel slightly fuzzy for a short time.

"Timmy Turner," began Seth officially. "You may recall, upon our meeting earlier today, that we made a little bet between ourselves." Timmy nodded and took another gulp of revolting beer. "Well," Seth continued, eyeing up Mr Poops, who was peering over the table top from Timmy's lap, "the results are in..."

Kha and Irsu started a drum roll on the table with their enormous hands. The noise was deafening and then suddenly stopped. There was a silence that seemed to go on for an eternity. Seth stood up and held his hand out to Timmy.

"Timmy Turner, I don't know how you did it, but I am now making you an honorary member of the Pyramid Builders' Association. Congratulations, young man."

Tears rolled down Timmy's cheeks and he smiled a big cheesy smile. He shook that giant hand with all his might and all his fear and self-doubt vanished. He picked up Mr Poops and did a little dance, holding him in the air and singing "We did it! We did it!"

"The workers are happy," continued Seth. "Fewer of them are collapsing and they have worked three times harder today. We are so impressed that we would like to keep your café as a permanent fixture."

"Wow!" said Timmy. "Thank you so much."

"No, thank you, Timmy. You have shown strength, courage and determination. You will go far in life young man. Here is your Pyramid Builders' Association Scarab. Wear it with pride." Seth handed Timmy a golden scarab beetle badge. It was beautiful. Timmy pinned it to his top immediately.

"Thank you, Seth. I will wear it proudly, every single day."

"Congratulations!" cheered the three brothers. "Welcome to the Association."

Seth smiled at Timmy as if he were his own son. "We would like you to stay here tomorrow, Timmy. We have some new workers coming to run the café and we need you to show them the ropes... and the food."

"It would be my pleasure," replied Timmy.

"Fantastic. Now, let's have a little celebration party! More beer, boys?"

Seth, Irsu and Kha had more beer, while Timmy had some fruit and bread. He found some oil lanterns that were in the cart and lit them. The five of them stayed up until late into the night, laughing, talking, singing and having a fantastic time.

Mr Poops may have had a sip or two of beer because he jumped onto the table and rolled around waiting for more tummy tickles, which the brothers were happy to provide.

Eventually, the three men decided it was time to go home. They thanked Timmy for his hospitality and staggered back towards the pyramid. They assured Timmy that their houses were on the other side – they just needed to remember which ones were theirs.

Timmy wished them luck and waved goodbye. It was starting to feel very cold so Timmy picked up Mr Poops and climbed into the cart where he found some leftover fabric from the build. He wrapped them both in the fabric, making

them look a bit like mummies, and they fell asleep beneath

the Ancient Egyptian stars.

Chapter Four

A few hours later, Timmy and Mr Poops were awoken by the sound of voices.

"Wakey wakey Mr Timmy. Ra is rising in the sky and it's time for us to get to work."

Timmy wearily opened one eye. Instantly struck by the intense sunlight, he closed it again. He slowly sat up, shielded his eyes and tried again. A row of three faces was staring at him over the side of the cart: two young girls and a young man.

"Good morning, Mr Timmy," they chirped. "We are here to learn the ways of your café."

For a moment, Timmy wondered where he was and if he was still dreaming. He looked at the little faces that were peering over the side of the cart, then he looked down at Mr Poops, who was still snoring next to him, and then he remembered yesterday's completely bonkers day and finally remembered where he was.

"Good morning," he yawned. "I'll be with you in two minutes. Please, go to the table and make yourselves comfortable."

The three workers did as they were told, and Timmy climbed down from the cart, followed by Mr Poops, who promptly found himself a shady spot beneath a tree and went back to sleep.

Timmy did his best to flatten his scruffy hair. He was bursting for the toilet after his evening with Seth and his brothers, and he had to hide behind the cart to relieve himself.

Feeling a little more human, he walked into the café, splashed his face and hands with some water that was in one of his washing-up buckets, and walked over to the table. He was amazed to see that the workers had already cleared up from last night's party, and they had even done the washing up.

'These three will be just fine,' he thought to himself as he sat down.

"Good morning, team. How nice to meet you," he said to the trio as they sat in front of him. "I'm Timmy Turner, honorary member of the Pyramid Builders' Association and founder of this café. Seth has asked me to teach you how everything works today, so that you can run the café for yourselves. Sadly, I have to leave here later this afternoon, but I can already see that you can manage the café with no problem at all."

The three workers looked very pleased with themselves.

"Please, tell me your names."

The boy spoke. "I am Dedi," he said, "and these are my sisters, Ana and Ipy."

"Welcome to you all," smiled Timmy. "How old are you?"

"Well, I am 12," replied Dedi. "Ana is 11 and Ipy is 10. We are fast learners and we work hard. Our father tells us that we are very clever."

"I'm sure that you are," said Timmy. "What is your father's name?"

"Our father is Kha," Dedi went on. "He's very impressed with your work, Timmy Turner."

Timmy blushed. "Well, I am very impressed with his work too. Those pyramids are spectacular. Right team, we'd better get on. We'll have a café full of hungry workers here very soon! Dedi, do you think you could go to the market with the ox and cart to collect fresh supplies? We need bread, fruit, water, beer and maybe some sausages." Out of the corner of his eye, Timmy saw Mr Poops twitch at the word 'sausages'.

"Yes, Mr Timmy. Right away," said Dedi as he left.

"Ana, please could you make sure all of the cups and plates are clean and the café is completely tidy and ready for the workers? And Ipy, do you think that you could collect a bit of firewood from the building site, and some stones? I have a plan."

"Yes, Mr Timmy. Of course," they chirped. And both set to work.

Timmy used Ipy's stones to build a circular stone fire pit outside the tent, and then he and Ipy made a fire using the wood she had collected. As the wood was so dry and the sun was already so hot, it took no time at all to make fire by rubbing two sticks together. All of those survival documentaries Timmy had watched with his dad were finally paying off. By the time Dedi returned, the fire was roaring and the café was ready to serve breakfast.

"Here is your order, Mr Timmy. Where would you like it?" Timmy directed Dedi, showing him where everything belonged and advising him to keep the sausages as cool as possible. Didi placed them in the shade under the counter, wrapped tightly in cloth.

"Okay everyone," Timmy announced, "it's important that we keep the café, and ourselves, clean. So please wash your hands in this bucket." Timmy held up a bucket of water and a small pot containing Egyptian soap, which he had found on the cart. "We need to wash our hands before we prepare any food." He demonstrated. "We wash them front and back, in between the fingers and under the nails. That's how my mother taught me, and she **always** knows best... that's what she tells me, anyway."

Dedi, Ipy and Ana did as they were told and, with clean hands, they set to work preparing fruit, laying the table and putting out the fresh bread. Meanwhile, Dedi started cooking sausages on sticks over the fire.

Mr Poops, who had been asleep throughout, suddenly awoke and followed his nose dreamily towards the delicious smell emanating from the fire.

He was not the only one to have smelt the sausages sizzling over the fire. Seth, Kha and Irsu appeared for breakfast. Timmy was quite surprised to see them looking so refreshed so early in the morning after the large volumes of beer they had consumed the previous night, but they all seemed remarkably well and they were all hungry. They sat at the table and tucked into the delicious food, while discussing their plans for the workers that day.

Kha beckoned Timmy over.

"Good morning, Timmy. We thought we'd come and see how you're getting on," said Kha as he ate his breakfast. "It looks like you are doing very well to me."

"Your children are very fast learners, Kha." said Timmy. "I think they will do a marvellous job here."

"So do I Timmy, thanks to all your hard work and imagination. You're certainly not scared of a challenge, are you?"

"I've enjoyed every minute," smiled Timmy. "Even those minutes when I was utterly terrified."

Kha looked Timmy in the eyes. "Sometimes, Timmy, we know we are doing something worthwhile because it fills us with fear. Imagine if nobody ever dared to do things differently: nothing would ever change. You have changed all our lives, Timmy Turner, with a simple solution."

"Often simple is best," replied Timmy.

Kha nodded in agreement. "That is certainly true, young man. As I always tell Seth, there is no need to overcomplicate the things we do, even when we are building the pyramids. Speaking of which, we'd better get back to work. As simple as they are, those pyramids won't build themselves you know." Kha finished his last piece of bread, stood up and then shook Timmy's hand. "It was an honour to meet you, Timmy Turner."

"Likewise," replied Timmy.

"Come on, boys," called Kha to his brothers. "Back to the grindstone."

The two giant brothers got up from the table and waved goodbye to Timmy. "Thanks for all your help," they called, and then they headed off towards the construction site.

"Any time," Timmy smiled, holding onto his Pyramid Builders' Association badge tightly and disappearing into a daydream about building his very own pyramid in his back garden.

"Mr Timmy! Mr Timmy!" His thoughts were interrupted by Ana tugging on his arm. "Mr Timmy, the men are coming for breakfast. Is everything ready?"

Timmy looked around his little café. Everything was perfect, just as he'd imagined when he came up with the plan yesterday. It was hard to believe that he and his friends had created all of this in just 24 hours, but they had done it. For a moment, he felt a very strange feeling – one that he barely recognised. It was pride. For once, Timmy felt proud of what he had achieved.

"Everything is fantastic, Ana. You are all doing a brilliant job. I'm very proud of you."

Ana looked a little embarrassed, and she smiled. "Thank you, Mr Timmy."

In no time at all, Timmy's café was once again filled with hungry workers eating their breakfast and chatting amongst themselves. The atmosphere was one of happiness and contentment.

As the day went on, Timmy supervised Dedi, Ipy and Ana, showing them other things that they might like to add to the café, like a sign and a menu of food symbols drawn onto a large stone outside the café so that the workers would know what was on offer.

He taught them how to organise breaks for themselves, how to stock-take and how to keep the café clean, tidy and organised. They were indeed fast learners, and Timmy felt sure that they would do a fantastic job.

As the day drew on, Timmy's thoughts began to return to his own situation and to his time-travelling toilet that was hidden away in the smelly public toilets at the market. He wondered what would happen when he flushed it this time. Then he began to worry. Timmy was very good at worrying. What if the toilet had vanished? What if it didn't work anymore? What if someone had discovered it in that dark corner... and used it? Yuck!

With the café running smoothly, Mr Poops full of sausages and scraps he had begged from the workers, and these thoughts swirling around in his head, Timmy decided that now would be a good time to head off on the next part of his adventure. He called his team to the counter.

"It's time I left now," he told them. "My father will need me at the farm and my mother will wonder where I've got to."

"We understand, Mr Timmy," said Ana. "It's a tough job being a child here, isn't it?"

"It certainly is," replied Timmy. "You have all worked incredibly hard. I know you will make a huge success of this café and the pyramid will be finished in no time."

"Hooray!" cheered the three children.

"I'm going back to the market for some fresh supplies," said Dedi. "Would you like a lift back on the cart?"

"Oh, yes please," said Timmy. He was feeling exhausted and quite nervous about the next part of his journey. That toilet seemed to have a mind of its own.

After saying goodbye to Ana and Ipy and waving to all the workers in the café, Timmy picked up Mr Poops and climbed into the cart, making himself comfortable on the fabric he had slept in. Dedi walked in front, leading the ox back towards the market, and Timmy took some time to enjoy the peace and take in the views of the vast sandy desert, the deep blue sky, and the new gleaming pyramids.

"That is just amazing," sighed Timmy to Mr Poops, who was snoring next to him.

Before long, they had reached the bustling market once more. The air was full of the calls of the market traders selling their wares and the smells of the foods, herbs, spices and perfumes that adorned their stalls. It was quite overpowering.

Dedi pulled up the cart in the shade of a fig tree, and a man immediately brought some food and water for the ox.

"Here we are, Timmy," Dedi called.

Timmy and Mr Poops jumped down from the cart. "Thank you so much for everything you have done, Dedi. Your father is right to be very proud of you. Good luck!"

"Good luck to you too, Mr Timmy."

The two boys waved goodbye and Timmy and Mr Poops made their way back through the market towards the building where their time-travelling toilet was hidden. They passed the baker with the gritty bread, the grocer with the whiffy onions and the lady who was selling the sweets.

"We're almost there," said Timmy to Mr Poops. But when he looked down, he realised that Mr Poops wasn't there. He was lost in the market!

Panic hit Timmy like a tidal wave. "Mr Poops," called Timmy. "MR POOPS!" His eyes darted around the market, desperately searching for his friend. He was nowhere to be seen. Timmy felt sick to his stomach.

Suddenly he heard a shout: "That dog has got my sausages! Stop him! THIEF!" And Timmy saw a flash of brown fur, which he believed to be Mr Poops, heading for the toilet block.

"Mr Poops," he scorned. "You are in BIG trouble!"

Timmy was right; Mr Poops was in big trouble. The angry butcher had formed a mob with the other market sellers and they were on the hunt for Mr Poops. Timmy ran towards the toilets and Mr Poops. He scooped Mr Poops up in his arms, a string of sausages hitting him in the face, and they darted into the dark doorway of the smelly toilet block. Timmy quickly headed for the corner where they had left the toilet the previous day. He could hear the angry crowd looking for Mr Poops outside.

"Where did he go?" asked one voice. "I dunno, but, when I find him, I'll turn that sausage dog into some tasty sausages!" said another, which Timmy presumed belonged to the butcher.

Timmy reached into the dark corner, and, to his relief, felt the familiar cold porcelain of his time-travelling toilet. Holding Mr Poops tightly, and flinging the sausages into the middle of the toilet block floor, Timmy grabbed the flush and pushed it upwards.

He heard another voice. "I wonder if he's hiding in the toilet."

"Please work," whispered Timmy, "please, please work."

"He'd be crazy to hide in that pongy stink pit!"

"Well, he is crazy! Crazy for upsetting the butcher, who could turn him into a nice sausage stew!"

Timmy heard footsteps entering the building. He pushed the flush upwards again in desperation. "Come on!" he whispered. "Take us away from here."

The footsteps were getting closer.

Timmy looked into the toilet. Bubbles were starting to appear – small, glittering bubbles – and then the colours began to return. They started swirling and swishing around in the toilet bowl.

"Aha! A trail of sausages," called the voice.

Timmy frantically pushed the lever upwards one more time, regretting throwing the sausages away and not letting Mr Poops eat the evidence. A dark figure appeared behind him. "Got you!" it cried. Timmy felt a hand tightly grip his arm. Then there was a huge flash of light and a loud bang. Timmy was swept off his feet by a large wave of colourful water and he and Mr Poops found themselves whizzing once more through the plumbing of time. They went twisting around

U-bends, sliding down multi-coloured pipework and flying

through the swirling water as fast as lightning – maybe even

faster. It was more fun than any water park he had ever

been to, even the one with the giant water slide that was

taller than his house. Timmy had never imagined that time

travel could be so much fun.

Then, suddenly, once again they came to an abrupt halt and

darkness descended.

Chapter Five

When his head had finally stopped spinning and the queasy feeling in his stomach had subsided, Timmy was able to focus on his surroundings. To his amazement, he could see trees and flowers and greenery in the most beautiful garden he'd ever set eyes upon. A warm summer breeze blew through his hair and the air was filled with birdsong, the buzzing of bumble bees and the heady scent of perfumed flowers. Timmy took a deep breath and inhaled the sweet smell of lavender and roses. It was a vast improvement on the hot, stinking toilet he'd just left in Ancient Egypt.

Mr Poops was clearly very happy to be here too, as Timmy turned around to see him relieving himself up a small fruit tree. "MR POOPS," Timmy cried, "you're such an animal!" Mr Poops put his nose in the air, turned his back on Timmy and began wandering around the paths that weaved in and out of the perfectly kept, symmetrical flowerbeds. He was obviously still upset about the sausage incident that had just occurred.

Timmy began to look around for some sort of clue as to where, and more importantly when, he was now. Admiring the green and pleasant land that surrounded him and the view across rolling hills and lush pastures, Timmy guessed that he may well be in England. He didn't have to wait long to find out, as he could hear a very loud and somewhat plummy voice heading in his direction reciting what Timmy thought must be some sort of poetry.

"There was a young girl from Bath,

Who always enjoyed a good laugh.

They sent her to me, and we joked about wee,

And we both wet our pants on the path!"

"Ha ha ha ha," scoffed the voice. "Oh no, no, NO! This is how I got into trouble in the first place. Try again, Sir Harington."

The man cleared his throat and continued...

"There was a young chap named John,

Who upset the Queen with his song.

She looked at his face, and called him a disgrace,

And declared 'One wants *that* one gone.'"

With that, the man burst into tears. Timmy felt terrible and

wondered if there was anything he could do to help. He was

feeling a little more confident now that he had helped the

Ancient Egyptians solve their problem.

Carefully sliding the time-travelling toilet behind a huge

purple wisteria that was growing by one of the garden walls,

Timmy and Mr Poops followed the sound of the wailing

through the beautiful, and now less peaceful, garden until

they saw a man sitting on a stone bench with a large, white

and slightly soggy handkerchief in his hand.

The man was dressed in a black tunic with big puffy

shoulders, black trousers, and black pointy shoes with shiny

buckles on them. Around his neck, he was sporting an

oversized white ruff that made him look a little bit like a

circus clown.

He had dark hair, a dark pointed beard and a moustache.

Timmy recognised the clothing as Elizabethan (he had seen it in his history book), but he didn't recognise the man.

By now, the sound of the wailing had become almost deafening. Slowly creeping closer, Timmy saw what looked like a notebook next to this eccentric character. On the front, he could see the words 'My Poetry – Keep Out!' written in black, splodgy ink. He guessed that this man must be some sort of poet – though, from what he'd just heard, he wasn't that sure.

"Are you alright?" Timmy asked softly.

The man lifted his head and looked at Timmy. "Splendid," he replied, loudly blowing his nose. "Never better."

"You don't *look* splendid," said Timmy.

"Charmed, I'm sure," came the reply. "As a matter of fact, I was being sarcastic. I feel absolutely darned atrocious," sniffed the man. "Anyway, why aren't you with the nanny? Is it her afternoon off?"

"The nanny?"

"Yes, you know, Nanny Effie. She's supposed to be keeping you all in check."

"Well, my nanny lives a long way from here."

"What are you talking about, boy? You *are* one of my children, aren't you?" Timmy stared blankly at the man. "When you have so many, it's very hard to keep tabs on all of them."

"Actually, sir, I'm not one of your children. My name is Timmy Turner and this is Mr Poops. We are world-famous explorers." Timmy had made that bit up, but he was sure that after this adventure they certainly would be. "I heard that you were upset and I thought we might be able to help you in some way?"

"World-famous, you say?" said the man, cheering up considerably. "How fantastic to meet a fellow celebrity. *I* am a world-famous poet. Or at least I was before my godmother, Liz, banished me to this terrible place where I have been forced to build my own shelter."

The man waved a hand in the direction of a huge Elizabethan manor house. It was beautiful – like one of the houses you see in period dramas at Christmas. It had pointed arches over the beautifully carved stone window

frames, the walls were draped with ivy and climbing roses and there was a tree-lined avenue leading to the enormous oak front door.

"Wow!" said Timmy. "You built that?"

"Well, Daddy and I had some people do it for us, with some plans from an Italian fellow, but I paid for it, so therefore I built it, correct?"

"I guess so," said Timmy, knowing that the builders of Ancient Egypt might have something to say about that. "If you don't mind me asking," said Timmy hesitantly, "what *is* your name? You're not William Shakespeare, are you?"

The man looked offended. "No, my dear boy. I am a *far* better poet and writer than that man will ever be, what with all those murders and ridiculous plays about bottoms! My name, as if you didn't already know, is Sir John Harington, poet and outstanding writer extraordinaire. I must read you one of my pieces at once..."

He cleared his throat and flicked through his battered notebook.

"Ah yes, here we are:

There was a young girl from Dorset,

Who had a spectacular corset.

It lit up the night, as it glittered so bright.

Then it blasted her off into orbit!"

Timmy looked at the man, unsure of what to say. The only John Harington he knew of was the man who had invented the first flushing toilet and later installed one for his godmother, Queen Elizabeth the First, at her palace. Then it all made sense. This *was* that John Harington; he'd been banished from the palace for his rude jokes and frankly terrible writing, and 'Godmother Liz' was in fact Her Royal Highness Queen Elizabeth the First!

"It's a privilege to meet you Mr... I mean Sir Harington," said Timmy as he sort of bowed and curtseyed at the same time.

Sir Harington was not paying attention, as he had been rifling through his poetry book in search of the perfect poem to perform for Timmy and Mr Poops.

"Ah ha!" he yelled triumphantly. "Here's a real belter for you..."

'Oh no,' thought Timmy. 'Not another one.'

"There was a young lady from France,

Who often would like a good dance.

She'd boogie to hits,

But she once did the splits

And she ripped a big hole in her pants!"

Timmy didn't know what to say. How was he supposed to respond to pants poetry? He clapped half-heartedly in an attempt to look like he'd enjoyed the recital. Sir Harington looked pleased with himself and was about to find another literary treat to read when Timmy interrupted.

"Is that a fountain I can hear?" As he followed the sound of trickling water, he saw a small fountain at the end of one of the neatly pruned pathways.

"Yes it is, you clever chap. I designed that myself. You see, the water is fed from the pond up there on the hill, through some pipes and all the way down to my fountain. I created so much pressure that the water shoots out like... well, like water out of a fountain!"

"That's very clever," said Timmy.

"I know," snorted Sir Harington. "And, on the top, I have placed a small statue of a hare, a ring and a tun, so that people know that it's all my own work."

Again, Timmy looked blankly at the man.

"Hare – ring – tun," he repeated. "Harington!"

"Oh, I see!" said Timmy. The puns were almost as bad as the poetry. "I love inventing things. My father and I are always making new inventions in our workshop."

"Oh, how fortunate our paths have crossed," said Sir Harington. "I love inventing too. I've been working on some more ideas in the house. You seem like the sort of chap who appreciates some decent plumbing. Would you like to see it?"

"Oh, yes please," said Timmy enthusiastically.

"My wife thinks I'm crazy," Sir Harington continued.

"I can't think why," Timmy uttered!

"Come along then. Your canine friend can have luncheon with my hounds, while we try and iron out the last little problems with my invention."

Mr Poops looked worried until he sniffed the smell of some rather fine sausages in the air. Then he happily followed Timmy and Sir Harington towards the manor house.

****

After leaving Mr Poops in a barn, happily munching through a large bowl of sausages, Timmy followed Sir Harington to the manor house. The door opened to reveal a spectacular country home. It was like walking into the pages of one of those Ideal Country Home magazines. Mrs Turner read them all the time and Timmy would often hear her sigh as she lifted her face from the pages to survey her own, less stately, more of a state, sort of home.

The entrance hall was a vast space with beautiful panelled walls, a hand-painted ceiling with golden leaves and deep red roses and a sparkling marbled floor. In front of Timmy was an enormous oak staircase that swept up and around to probably at least 12 bedrooms. It was breathtaking.

"Welcome to my shelter," announced Sir Harington.

"I've never seen anything like it."

"I know," sighed Sir Harington. "It's terribly tricky to live in such a tiny house on a daily basis, especially when you have so many children and staff."

"How many children have you got?"

"Oh, I don't know, somewhere between nine and fifteen. They are all with Nanny Effie or off at boarding school, so it's hard to keep track. I only really see them all at Christmas."

"Oh," said Timmy. He knew he would feel really sad if he only ever saw his dad at Christmas.

"Would you like a quick bite to eat before we go and see my latest invention? I think Cookie has been baking her best tarts again."

Timmy was quite hungry now. After all, he hadn't eaten for centuries! "Yes please," he replied.

"Fabulous! Follow me then dear chap."

Sir Harington led Timmy through a huge banqueting hall and several smaller, but equally opulent, rooms full of beautiful antique furniture and ceramics, though it occurred to Timmy that these were not antiques at all – they were in fact ultra-modern for their time, as was the rest of the manor house.

At the back of the house, they came to a kitchen where a rather rotund lady with wild hair and ruddy cheeks was clearly cooking up a storm. Pots and pans were clanging, steam was rising from tureens, an open fire was crackling with a pot bubbling above it, and a large dresser was already covered in plates of what looked like biscuits and tarts.

"Cookie!" yelled Sir Harington over the din. "This is my new chum, Timmy Turner. He's a world-famous explorer, don't you know? Do you think we could have some of your delicious apple tart and perhaps a glass of wine?"

Cookie raised her head from the pan she was stirring and looked Sir Harington up and down. "Well, don't tell Lady Harington then," she replied in a strong west-country accent. "She'll have my guts for garters if she knows you're sneaking in here eating apple tart and drinking her wine. After all, you have got to get into those tights and trousers for the banquet tonight haven't you, little piggy."

"Ah. Yes, yes…" replied Sir Harington, patting his potbelly.

"We'll just have a little taster." And he held out a plate.

"I don't think I can drink wine," interrupted Timmy.

"Really? Why ever not?" shrieked Sir Harington in surprise.

"I thought everyone could drink wine." And he took a large slurp from the glass that Cookie had just passed him to prove his point.

"Well, I'm only young," said Timmy, "my mother won't approve. I'll just have water."

Sir Harington spat out his wine and it sprayed across the kitchen like a sprinkler!

"My dear boy, if you drink our water you will surely die! This is part of the reason for my latest invention. Here, have some ale. All my children drink ale. It's much safer that way."

So, grabbing his apple tart and a mug of ale, Timmy followed Sir Harington through the house until they reached a door with a sign on it that read "water closet".

This is it, thought Timmy. This is the invention that will one day change the lives of millions of people.

"Are you ready to witness a spectacular invention, the likes of which you have never seen before?" bellowed Sir Harington, his hand outstretched ready to open the door.

"Yes!" cried Timmy excitedly.

Sir Harington turned the handle and flung back the door.

"Fanfare please," he yelled. "Behold, my greatest invention of all time... Ajax!"

There in front of Timmy was a very primitive-looking toilet. If he didn't know any better, he would have thought it was a hole in a plank of wood. But Timmy did know better: he could see a cistern that contained water for flushing, as well as a small knob that allowed the toilet to flush when you twisted it, and also a toilet bowl – rather than a hole in the floor.

"Wow!" said Timmy. "That's very impressive, Sir Harington. You are indeed a very fine inventor."

"Why, thank you my dear boy. That's very kind of you to say so. I created this as a prototype for my dear Godmother Liz in an attempt to get her to forgive me for my inappropriate writings. She really dislikes the smelly privies in her castles and she is desperate for a solution... so here it is!"

Timmy couldn't help but notice that there was still a pretty nasty smell coming from the toilet and he looked at Sir Harington to see if he had noticed.

"What is it that you are struggling with, Sir Harington?" he enquired.

"Well, my trouble is that I promised dear Liz that I would make unsavoury places smell sweet, noisome places wholesome and filthy places sweetly. As you may have noticed, there is still somewhat of a whiff around my invention, and, even though I have it emptied every day, I cannot seem to stop the rancid smell. Do you have any thoughts?"

Timmy thought for a moment. "As a matter of fact," he said, "I do."

"Oh, thank goodness!" cried Sir Harington. "I do so miss those parties at the palace."

"I think that your invention is amazing," said Timmy. "But there are two things that could make it even better. First of all, have you ever considered covering the seat with a lid?"

"A lid? Well, then wouldn't one tinkle on the lid and splash one's feet?"

"No, Sir Harington. This lid is on a hinge, so you lift it to do your business and then replace it before you flush to stop the smell rising up one's nostrils."

"By Jove, my dear boy! You are a genius!"

Timmy was taken aback by this comment. "My teacher says I'm an idiot," said Timmy quietly. "She thinks my inventions are a waste of time and I won't get anywhere if I don't know all of my times tables off by heart."

"Well Timmy, I think that your teacher is a dulcop, a fopdoodle, a skelpie-limmer and a total dorbel."

"I have no idea what you just said!" giggled Timmy.

"A dorbel, a nincompoop, a petty, nitpicking teacher. She doesn't deserve to have your talents in her classroom, and don't you ever forget that."

Timmy felt a little emotional after such high praise. "Would you like to hear my second idea?" he asked.

"Yes! Oh yes! Absolutely."

"Well," said Timmy. "Having been in your beautiful garden, I did notice that there was the most amazing smell of lavender and roses out there."

"Are you suggesting I put my invention in the garden?" asked Sir Harington.

"No, no! I'm suggesting that you cut a few stems of lavender and roses and place them in here. Their scent may go some way to freshen the air. Call it an air freshener, if you will."

Sir Harington was looking astounded!

"My dear chap. You are a wonder. Godmother Liz is going to love my Ajax invention."

"Can I just ask," said Timmy. "Why have you called it Ajax?"

"Well, I'm glad you asked," replied Sir Harington. "It's one of my fabulous jokes. When the folks around here need to go to the toilet, they often say they are going for a jakes. So I have put a little twist on that phrase and called it the Ajax."

"Oh," smiled Timmy, raising his eyebrows. "Now it makes perfect sense."

"Well, one doesn't want one's name yelled out every time someone needs to tinkle. Imagine people yelling, 'I'm just popping to the Harington!' or, worse, 'I'm desperate for the John!'. That would be simply awful!"

Timmy thought it best not to say any more. Instead, he just nodded in agreement.

"Timmy, I would really like to thank you properly for your help – perhaps you would like to join us tonight at the banquet? It's just a few friends from the palace and so on. I'd be overjoyed if you would stay. You are, of course, welcome to sleep over in one of our bedrooms. I'll have the housekeeper make one up for you."

The chance to stay and banquet in this beautiful house was something that Timmy could not turn down. "I'd love to," he replied, without any hesitation.

"Splendid!" cheered Sir Harington. "I'll ring for the housekeeper at once. Prudence! Prudence, where are you?" Sir Harington pulled at a lever in the hall, which must have made a bell ring somewhere else in the enormous mansion. He waited to hear the steps of the housekeeper.

"Prudence is such a lovely girl," he told Timmy. "She hales from Cornwall, poor thing, but she really is very nice."

"Cornwall is a beautiful place," said Timmy, "full of rugged coastline and tiny villages."

"Oh really?" said Sir Harington, sounding surprised.

"Perhaps I should go there then."

"Yes, you really should."

They were interrupted by a soft Cornish accent. "You called, sir?"

Timmy turned around to see a tall, thin, dark-haired lady standing at the bottom of the stairs. She was wearing a long grey dress that was covered by a white apron. Her hair was pulled back into a tight bun and she looked very neat and tidy.

"Ah, Prudence. There you are. This is Timmy Turner. He is a world-famous explorer and my new friend. He will be joining me this evening for the banquet. Would you be so kind as to make him up a room and maybe find him something more suitable to wear for dinner? I'm sure there are plenty of hand-me-downs in the nursery – that's one of the joys of having so many children."

"Of course, Sir Harington. Right away."

"Fabulous, thank you Prudence. Timmy, I will leave you in Prudence's capable hands and will see you later on for pre-dinner drinky-poos!" And, with that, he turned and skipped away towards the kitchen.

Chapter Six

"This way, Master Turner," said Prudence as she led him up the stairs to the third floor of the manor house. It was quite a long climb and Timmy's legs ached by the time they reached the top. Prudence, however, had no such trouble.

At the top of the stairs, a long, door-lined corridor stretched to the left and right. Timmy thought that he had better take note of where he was so he could find his room again later. Prudence turned right and walked all the way along to the last door on the left. "This is my favourite room," she said. "It has lovely views out across the gardens." She opened the door and Timmy walked in.

"Wow!" he gasped as he took in the spectacular sight.

The first thing Timmy noticed was the beautiful high-vaulted ceiling. It was decorated in ornate plasterwork, which criss-crossed the roof. There was an enormous four-poster bed at one end of the room, complete with sumptuous green curtains. The same style curtains were lavishly draped around the two tall windows, which looked across the country estate.

On either side of the bed were two carved wooden tables with a candle on each. In one corner of the room was a large wooden chest of drawers and at the foot of the bed was a huge blanket box. Looking at the floor, Timmy also noticed a beautiful blue and green rug and he immediately took off his shoes.

"There's no need to do that, Master Turner," said Prudence. "You'll get a draught on your toes through these floorboards."

"Please, call me Timmy," replied Timmy. "This really is a beautiful room."

"Yes, it is," smiled Prudence. "I'll fetch some sheets and make up this bed for you and then we'll see about finding you something to wear for the banquet."

Timmy sat on the window seat and gazed out onto the enchanting gardens and countryside. In the distance, he could see a small church that he guessed must be in the local village. Prudence returned with an armful of sheets and blankets and set about making up the bed. Timmy continued to look out at the gardens. He could see Sir Harington walking around and waving his arms dramatically in the air, like he was chasing away an irritating wasp. He giggled and Prudence peered over his shoulder.

"He's reciting that terrible poetry again," she laughed. "He's probably preparing something special for the banquet tonight. You're in for a treat, Timmy Turner!" They both took a moment to marvel at the sight before Prudence said: "Right, your bed is made, there's a chamber pot underneath in case nature calls in the middle of the night, and I will come and light these candles before you go to bed."

"Thank you, Prudence. That's so kind of you," said Timmy.

"Don't mention it," she smiled. "We'd better go and find you something to wear for the banquet, young man. Follow me." And, once again, Prudence led him through the house. This time, they went past the staircase to a room at the other end of the long corridor.

Stepping into this room, Timmy could see that this was the children's nursery. It was full of toys that looked very expensive indeed. Hand-painted, wooden toy soldiers were on parade on one of the shelves, and there were beautiful dolls, bows and arrows, fishing rods, marbles and board games. And, yet, there were no children.

"Where are all the children?" asked Timmy.

"Well, the boys are away at boarding school and the girls are out with Nanny Effie. They will be home later."

"Oh," said Timmy. "Why aren't the girls at school? Are they ill?"

Prudence burst out laughing. "Girls? At school! What a ridiculous notion! What would girls need to go to school for? I don't know where you've come from, Timmy Turner, but I've never heard of such poppycock as girls at school."

Timmy then remembered that of course girls didn't go to school in Elizabethan times. These girls were lucky to have a nanny who would teach them a few things, but mainly they would just be taught how to be ladies and homemakers.

"Of course," he yawned. "I think I'm a bit tired. I'm only just back from Egypt and it was a very long journey."

"I think you might be right," agreed Prudence. "Now then, let's find you some clothes and then you can go and have a nice rest in your room before dinner. You can get changed behind that screen over there. I'll find you some things that might fit you."

Timmy did as he was told and went behind the screen. He listened as Prudence rummaged through the children's hand-me-downs, muttering to herself: "Too big. Too small. Oh no! Too itchy... Ah ha! This might be just the thing." Suddenly, a pair of woollen tights and some peacock-blue velvet trousers appeared over the top of the screen.

"Try those on," called Prudence. "I'll have a look for the rest of it."

Timmy had never worn a pair of tights before and he had no idea how to put them on. He tried pulling them onto his feet, like socks, but that didn't work because his feet got stuck and the ends of the tights went all floppy. He tried putting them on while standing up, but he fell over. He even

tried putting his arms in first to stretch the wool, but that

just made the material a bit baggy. Eventually, he managed

to sit down, roll the tights down, push in his feet and wiggle

the tights up. They were a bit itchy.

Next were the short trousers. Being a slip of a boy, these

went on with relative ease, but the trouble was that they

kept falling down. There was no belt or button on them.

"Are you alright round there?" called Prudence.

"Yes," replied Timmy. "Except I don't seem to be able to

hold my trousers up."

"That's because you need a doublet, Timmy."

"A what-let?"

"A doublet. Here!"

A white shirt and a blue velvet jacket were flung over the

top of the screen. Timmy put on the shirt and tucked it into

his itchy tights. He noticed that the jacket, apparently called

a doublet in these times, had strings attached to the inside

waistband. His trousers had hoops of fabric. They must tie

together, he concluded – and indeed they did. He fastened his doublet buttons and was about to step out when he heard Prudence say, "Two more things."

A hand appeared around the screen holding a large white ruff and a pair of black shiny shoes, which had tiny heels and big brass buckles on the front.

Timmy put on the shoes and then looked at the ruff. He had no idea how to put that on. What was it even for? Maybe it was to catch bits of his dinner in later, like some sort of flamboyant bib.

"How are you getting on, young man?" called Prudence.

"I'm having some trouble with my ruff," replied Timmy.

"Come out here and I'll help you. They can be very tricky indeed."

Timmy stepped out from behind the screen and Prudence looked at him, like a mum looks at her baby on their first day of school.

"Very smart, Timmy Turner. Very smart indeed," she said. Then she took the ruff, fastened it from behind and stepped back to admire her work. Timmy didn't like the ruff one bit.

Now he knew how Mr Poops had felt that time when he had

had an operation at the vets and he'd had to wear that

crazy lampshade around his neck. Poor Mr Poops.

"Well, don't you look a proper gentleman!" beamed

Prudence like a proud mother.

Timmy stood still, trying not to itch through his tights. He

quite liked his new look, apart from the ridiculous ruff, and

he felt a little bit like a character in a school play, though he

knew that this was no act. The thought that he was in an

actual Elizabethan manor house, dressed in a peacock-blue

suit, getting ready to have an authentic Elizabethan

banquet, was almost making his brain explode with

excitement.

"What do you think, Timmy?" asked Prudence.

"Well, it's not my usual choice of outfit, that's for sure, but I

really like it. Thank you for finding it for me."

"No trouble at all, Master Turner. Now, you could probably do with a rest before the banquet. I'll take you back to your room for some peace."

"Thank you, Prudence. That would be lovely."

They made their way back through the house to Timmy's room, where he enjoyed an hour of total peace and quiet sat on the window seat watching the birds and butterflies dance around the garden; it was most relaxing. As the bells on the church tower clock chimed five, Timmy thought that he should go and check on Mr Poops. Leaving his room and making a mental note of its precise location, Timmy wandered through the house and down the stairs, through the entrance hall and out of the large oak door to the garden. He headed towards the barn where he had left Mr Poops earlier.

Peering around the door, he saw Mr Poops stretched out on a bale of hay. There were hunting dogs in the barn who looked somewhat livelier than Mr Poops – perhaps they hadn't eaten quite so many sausages, thought Timmy. Mr Poops lifted his head and looked at Timmy curiously. After a leisurely yawn and a big stretch, Mr Poops sauntered over to his master, looked him up and down and began to sniff at the black shiny shoes. Timmy could have sworn that he saw Mr Poops snigger at him – he wondered if it was even possible to have a sniggering sausage dog.

He gave Mr Poops a tickle on the tummy. "Have you eaten lots of sausages, my little sausage dog?" he cooed. Mr Poops jumped up on his hind legs and licked Timmy's nose, before returning to his cosy spot amongst the hay.

Reassured that his friend was perfectly fine, he was about to make his way back to the house when he heard the clip-clop of horses' hooves on the driveway. That must be the first guests arriving, he thought. Looking down the tree-lined avenue, he could see a carriage being drawn by two beautiful black horses. He watched as it drew closer; it was like a scene from one of those period dramas.

At the top of the driveway, the horses stopped and a coachman opened the door of the carriage. Out stepped a beautiful lady in a long crimson Elizabethan dress. It was laced with golden yellow cuffs and she was wearing a matching headdress with her hair perfectly arranged. A man emerged from the carriage looking equally grand in a yellow velvet suit, not dissimilar in style to the one Timmy was wearing.

A butler appeared at the door of the house to greet the guests and he took them inside. As Timmy looked down the avenue, he could see other carriages arriving, so he decided he should return to the house.

On entering the large hallway, he could hear some beautiful

music coming from one of the downstairs rooms. He

followed the sound to the drawing room, where he found Sir Harington – now dressed in an indigo-blue suit – talking to his guests in his usual flamboyant way. He stopped mid-sentence and looked at Timmy.

"Ah ha! Timmy Turner! Well, don't you look smart? Please do come in, young man." Sir Harington beckoned Timmy towards him, and Timmy followed. "Come and meet my friend Walter Raleigh. Have you met before? He's in a similar line of work to you, exploring far-flung places and all that."

Timmy's mouth fell open. He couldn't believe it – he was standing in a room and about to shake hands with THE Sir Walter Raleigh. The actual real life one! He looked up at the tall man standing in front of him and held out his hand. "It's an honour to meet you, sir," he said. "I've followed your work and travels with great interest."

"Why, thank you," replied Walter in a soft Devonshire accent. "I'm sorry, but I've not heard of you before Timmy."

"No, you won't have heard of me," said Timmy. "I've been in Egypt for quite a while. Only just got back."

"Wow! That's a big adventure for someone so young," said Walter in admiration.

"Yes," replied Timmy, "it certainly was!"

Their meeting was interrupted as the doors to the room swung open and the butler announced the arrival of some more guests. "Sir Robert Dudley and his wife Lettice Knollys."

"Ahhhh! It's Dudders!" yelled Sir Harington. "Dudders, you old fool. How the devil are you?" and he ran across the hall to meet his friend. Robert and Sir Harington shook hands and then did a funny little dance. It was clearly an 'in joke', because they found it utterly hilarious. Timmy could see Robert's wife, Lettice, rolling her eyes as she watched them from a distance.

More and more guests arrived and Timmy concluded that many of them were friends from Queen Elizabeth's court, where Sir Harington had worked before getting himself banished for telling rude jokes and for his terrible writing. The room was filling with people. They were all talking and laughing as the music played. This was surely more than 'just a few friends', Timmy thought. After a while, the doors opened again and the butler announced: "Lady Harington, wife of Sir John Harington."

Timmy looked up, intrigued to see this lady. Sir Harington looked up, slightly nervously. In walked a tall, slender woman wearing a black dress that was embroidered with gold. Around her neck, she wore a large ruff.

"My darling Mary," cried Sir Harington, heading over to greet his wife. "How are you? I haven't seen you all day." He kissed the back of her hand.

Mary fixed Sir Harington with an icy stare. "No rude poetry tonight, please," she said in a whispered tone.

"No dear," smiled Sir Harington. "Ladies," he announced to the guests, "my wife Mary would love to escort you outside for drinks on the terrace before dinner. Please do follow her."

All of the finely dressed ladies made their way out of the room behind Lady Harington, towards the terrace.

"Phew!" cried Sir Harington when they had all gone.

"Anyone for a drink?"

All the men cheered. The butler appeared with a tray of glasses and some bottles of wine and he set about pouring drinks for all the gentlemen. Timmy thought it best not to drink wine and so he just ate some delicious canapés that were spread around the room on little plates. There was a real party atmosphere as Sir Harington entertained his friends with wild stories and fabulous music. Timmy wanted to enjoy every colourful moment and store it in his memory forever.

Just as Sir Harington was regaling his audience with another wild story – this time about the time he'd had an unfortunate incident with a tiger and a pork chop at the palace – the doors opened once more and a huge gong was sounded by a wild-looking Cookie, who yelled in her best west-country accent, "DINNER IS SERVED!"

Timmy was starving and he watched as the finely dressed ladies and gentlemen made their way to the banqueting hall. Their clothes were a rainbow of extravagance, which told Timmy that these people were all very well to do indeed. He recalled that, in Elizabethan times, the colours of your clothing were also a display of your wealth and status. He followed along behind the very wealthy crowd.

Nothing could have prepared him for the sight that greeted him. The hall was lit with candles and the table was a work of art. What appeared to be a green lawn spread from one end of the table to the other, winding its way between delicate plates and cutlery. Vast quantities of food filled this landscape, decorated with peacock feathers, flowers and foliage, which were also woven around sparking glassware and twinkling candles. It was like something from a fairy tale.

The guests found their places and stood to await their hosts. Timmy found his place at the far end of the table, in between Sir Harington (who was, of course, head of the table) and Robert Dudley, whom he had seen earlier.

"Sir Harington and his wife Lady Harington," announced the butler. The room erupted in applause as the Haringtons placed themselves at either end of the table.

"Please be seated," called Sir Harington. "Let the banquet begin!"

Music started to play once more and Timmy noticed that a small band of musicians had now set up in a corner of the room. He looked at his plate and saw that, on it, was a menu of all the food on the table. It read:

Civet of hare

¼ stag

Stuffed chicken

Loin of veal covered in sugar plums and pomegranate seeds

Meat pie

Stuffing

Hard-boiled eggs with saffron and cloves

It's a bit meat-heavy, Timmy thought, but he wasn't that keen on vegetables anyway.

Suddenly, the room filled with waiters and waitresses who started serving food and drinks to all the guests. Timmy's plate began to be piled high with various dishes he'd never eaten or even heard of before.

"Would you like some pie?" asked a waitress.

"What's in it?"

"Chicken and gravy…"

"Oh, yes please," said Timmy. He knew where he was with chicken and gravy.

"I've not finished," she went on, "and deer and goose and pigeon and capon and rabbit."

"Ah!" said Timmy. "I think I'll pass, thank you." Indigestion was not something he wanted to have in the 1500s – he doubted very much that he would like any remedy from the time. It would probably be some concoction made of slug slime and stinging nettles.

"Tuck in, Timmy!" said Sir Harington rather loudly. He was clearly having a fantastic time and it was obvious to Timmy that he quite liked being the centre of attention.

Timmy ate his way through everything on his plate, even the bits he was unsure of. It was actually surprisingly tasty. By the time his plate was cleared away, he was stuffed full, but, to his astonishment, no sooner was the table cleared than more food was put in its place. Timmy was given a clean plate with another menu. This menu read:

Roe deer

Roasted pig

Sturgeon cooked in parsley, vinegar and ginger

Goat

Goose

Chicken

Pigeon

Rabbit

Heron

Wild boar

It looked like an inventory of the local nature reserve, rather

than a menu, and, once more, Timmy noticed a distinct lack

of fruit and vegetables. This time, he was much more

choosey about what was on his plate, preferring to stick to

meat that he was familiar with, rather than eating the entire

cast of a wildlife documentary.

Sir Harington was stuffing his beardy chops as though he'd

never eaten before. "Would you like some ale, young man?"

he asked Timmy.

Timmy nodded his head and held out his glass. He was going

to need something to wash all this food down. "Are you

enjoying yourself, Timmy?" asked Sir Harington.

Timmy was having the time of his life. "Yes, I certainly am,"

he replied. "This is the best party I've ever been to!"

"I do like a good party," cheered Sir Harington, raising his glass in the air. "Cheers to one and all!" he yelled.

"CHEERS!" came the slightly tipsy reply of everyone around the table.

Timmy managed to eat some of the food on his plate. He wrapped a chicken leg and a bit of pork in a napkin and wedged it into his pocket to take to Mr Poops later. He was feeling absolutely full to the brim – the sort of full up that you get after Christmas dinner, where everyone shuffles away from the table loosening their belts and declaring that their diet will begin in the new year. Timmy was very grateful for his baggy-waisted trousers.

Again, when everyone had finished, the table was cleared and more food was sent from the kitchen.

"How many courses are there?" Timmy asked Robert Dudley, who was sat on his right.

"Oh, not many. Only five this time."

"FIVE!" cried Timmy.

"Yes. Money's a bit tight for John since he was banished from the court at the palace. His banquets are not what they once were."

"I see."

Timmy tried to imagine an even more extravagant meal than this, but it was almost impossible.

A clean bowl and the next menu arrived. This course was much shorter than the first two and the menu read:

Wafers

Red and white jelly

Maybe I could fit in a wafer, Timmy thought, as the next round of spectacular food arrived at the table. He reached over, took a wafer and nibbled the edges like a little mouse.

"Aren't you hungry, Timmy Turner?" enquired Sir Harington.

"I'm a little full at the moment," said Timmy. "What with all this wonderful food, I fear my eyes may be bigger than my belly."

"Yes, I struggle with that problem too," chuckled Sir Harington. "We should have a little interlude to let our food go down." He tapped his glass with a spoon, stood up on his chair and bellowed "Ladies and gentlemen." The room fell silent. "I feel it is time for you to enjoy a little poetic interlude – a piece I wrote just yesterday, in fact."

Everyone at the table cheered. Timmy wondered if they had ever actually heard their host's poetry before. Sir Harington cleared his throat and began.

"Dear friends and family member (that's you, Mary),

One hopes that you will remember,

Dear Godmother Lizzy,

Who's gone a bit dizzy,

And banished this marvellous pretender (that's me!)."

"BOO! What a meanie!" cried all the guests. Sir Harington

played up to his audience by pulling sad faces and

pretending to cry before he went on.

"I've had years of this frugal existence,

Queen Liz has kept me at a distance.

So I invented the loo,

To dispatch of her poo,

It was tricky and needed persistence.

One day I'll go back to the palace,

And make all my critics quite jealous.

With my new invention, I have every intention,

Of Lizzy becoming quite zealous."

For a moment, everyone looked at him blankly.

"(In other words, she'll love it!)," whispered Sir Harington to

the crowd.

The room went wild! They clapped and whooped and

cheered with gusto. They clearly loved this man and his

terrible poetry. The last bit barely rhymed but they didn't care. "More!" they cried. "More!"

Timmy concluded that the wine they were drinking must have some sort of mind-changing quality to it. Sir Harington jumped up onto the table. "Okay, okay, here's a joke for you," he giggled. "Why did Shakespeare visit the doctor?"

"We don't know. Why did Shakespeare visit the doctor?" retorted the guests.

"Because he was feeling a little ruff!" laughed Sir Harington, pulling at the ruff around his own neck.

Well, you would have thought that he'd just told the funniest joke in the world. The diners were falling about all over the place, some were doubled over holding their bellies, some had tears rolling down their faces and a few were rolling around on the floor. It was quite a spectacle to behold.

Amidst all the chaos and hysteria, the table had been cleared and plates changed for course four. Timmy read the menu.

Fruit tarts

Apple and cream pies

Cheese

Strawberries and plums stewed in rose water

It looked delicious and Timmy had almost got his appetite

back, when, suddenly, Sir Harington, who was now

completely carried away, decided to tell another joke.

"Knock knock," he roared.

"Who's there?" cried the giggling guests.

"Food."

"Food who?"

"FOOD FIGHT!" he yelled, picking up an apple and cream pie

and hurling it with all his might to the other end of the

table, where it hit a fairly portly-looking gentleman squarely

in the face.

The room fell silent. Lady Harington stood up and left the room. She looked utterly furious. Timmy watched in astonishment to see what would happen next.

The pie-faced man wiped the cream from his beard, licked his fingers and stood up. He picked up a fruit tart from a plate in front of him, took aim and launched it back in the direction of Sir Harington, who had realised he had gone too far and was gingerly climbing down from the table, unaware of what was coming.

The tart hit him splat on the bottom. Sir Harington let out a little yelp! All eyes were fixed on his posterior.

He slowly turned around and looked at his friends with a mischievous grin. They knew what to do. They all leaned forwards and grabbed a handful of pudding, still in total silence.

Timmy watched. He couldn't quite believe what he was witnessing. A room full of grown-ups behaving like children. It was hilarious, to say the least.

Sir Harington raised his pudding-free hand and broke the silence. "On your marks."

The guests changed their stances as if they were about to lunge into a race.

"Get set." All arms were drawn back, ready to fire.

"FOOD FIGHT!" squealed Sir Harington.

All at once, the band started playing and the air was full of flying puddings. Strawberries and plums whizzed past Timmy's ears like bullets and fruit tarts were being thrown like frisbees. Timmy had to duck to dodge a flying apple pie! This was the best dinner party Timmy had ever seen. Guests were giggling and wiping the cream and fruit from their faces before launching their next attack. Their grandiose surroundings were being totally destroyed – expensive vases were being smashed by flying cheeses and portraits of Sir Harington's ancestors were being splattered with jam and squashed plums. These people were having the time of their lives.

Suddenly, Timmy felt a hand grip his leg from beneath the table. It was Robert Dudley.

"Quick, boy!" he giggled. "Take cover!"

Timmy crawled under the table where Mr Dudley was hiding. "This is the safest place in the room," he told Timmy. "A good spot to regroup and gather more ammunition." Robert showed Timmy a plate full of cream-covered tarts he had collected from the table. "On my say so, we should crawl to the other end of the table, leap out and launch an attack on the enemy," he said in a military fashion. "The element of surprise will be our best weapon."

Timmy couldn't really argue. A fully-grown Elizabethan gentleman leaping out from under a table and hurling a cream and fruit tart in your face would certainly be a surprise – well, to most normal people anyway, although Timmy was beginning to question the definition of 'normal' in Sir Harington's house. Nonetheless, he did as he was told and followed Robert Dudley in an army crawl to the far end

. of the extremely long dining table. As planned, they emerged.

"Go! Go! Go!" cried Robert as Timmy scrambled to his feet and grabbed a weapon from the plate. He scanned the room for a target and there, right in front of him, was Walter Raleigh removing a squashed strawberry from his oversized ruff. Timmy couldn't resist. He drew back his arm and catapulted the pudding towards Walter Raleigh. It hit with a splat, right on his nose. Timmy fell about laughing.

"I say!" cried Walter. He reached behind him and, before Timmy knew it, a large squashy plum was dripping down his cheek. If his parents had seen the state of him, and indeed all of the party guests, they would have all been sent for baths and bedtime immediately, but his parents were hundreds of years in the future, so Timmy made the most of every delicious moment.

When all of the food from the table had been smeared over the room and the visitors, Sir Harington once again stood on the table and tapped his glass.

"Well, that's pudding done!" he sniggered. "Who's for wine and pastries on the terrace?"

Everyone cheered.

"Chivers, please open the doors," called Sir Harington to the butler, who had been dutifully watching the chaos from the corner of the room. He opened some tall glass doors at the side of the hall and the guests spilled out onto the lawn for yet more wine and food.

The sun was beginning to set and, after a bit of mingling and small talk, Timmy took the opportunity to sneak off and give Mr Poops the dinner he had stuffed in his pocket earlier. Leaving the party behind him, Timmy made his way to the barn, where he found Mr Poops sniffing at the hay. He looked very pleased to see Timmy and he licked the cream and fruit from his face with a big doggy kiss.

"Ahhhh, Mr Poops! I missed you too," smiled Timmy. He gave Mr Poops his snack, which he gulped down in two seconds flat, before lying on his back for a little tummy tickle.

The two friends had really missed each other and so Timmy decided that he would sneak Mr Poops back to his room to sleep. After all, part of the house had already been destroyed by flying puddings, so the presence of a sausage dog would surely go unnoticed.

Timmy listened to the sounds of the happy guests and the joyful music drifting on the soft night air. He could hear Sir Harington reciting yet more of his terrible poetry and he smiled. What an unforgettable night. Picking up Mr Poops, Timmy headed around the edge of the party and back through the open door into the hallway. Tucking Mr Poops under his doublet, he made his way back to his room.

He arrived to find the candles lit, as promised, and the bed covers turned down. He thought that perhaps he should have a wash before he climbed into the clean sheets, so he went to the wash stand to clean off the bits of pudding that Mr Poops had missed. Feeling fresher and a lot less sticky, he removed all of his Elizabethan clothes, including the incredibly itchy tights, placed them neatly on the blanket box and put on his own T-shirt. "Ahhh, that's better," he sighed.

He made quick use of his chamber pot before climbing into bed. The bed was so comfortable that Timmy sank into the feather mattress like he was lying on a cloud. Mr Poops jumped up next to him and, together, the two adventurers and best friends fell fast asleep.

****

Timmy awoke very early the next morning, just as the birds began their dawn chorus. He felt amazing. He'd had the best sleep of his life and now he was ready to continue on his journey through time. Waking Mr Poops, Timmy put on the rest of his clothes and his comfy old shoes, made his bed and tiptoed towards the door carrying a very sleepy Mr Poops. He suspected that some of the partygoers may be feeling rather tired and a bit under the weather after their extravagant banquet, so he made sure that he was extra quiet as he made his way downstairs and out of the house. Stepping out into the cool morning air, Timmy noticed that several guests were strewn across the lawn, still covered in pudding and fast asleep. He wanted to find Sir Harington to say goodbye, but he couldn't see him.

Timmy headed back towards the formal garden where he'd left his time-travelling toilet the day before. Walking past a large bush, he heard a moaning sound, so he stopped to take a closer look. "Aughhhh!" it moaned again.

"Hello?" said Timmy. "Who's in there?"

The bush shook and a voice whispered, "It's me, Sir Harington. Please turn off the lights, it's awfully bright."

"There are no lights," giggled Timmy, "you are in a bush in the garden."

"Oh, am I?" came the confused reply, followed by, "Oh yes, so I am. I'm coming out."

Timmy watched as a rather bedraggled Sir Harington crawled out from under the bush.

"Oh no!" he gasped.

"What is it?" questioned Timmy, a little panicked.

"Red sky," said Sir Harington, pointing towards the beautiful sunrise.

"Yes," said Timmy. "The sun is coming up."

"Don't you know the saying?" asked a horrified Sir Harington.

"No."

"Red sky at night, shepherds' delight. Red sky in the morning… you're up far too early, go back to bed."

Now he thought about it, Timmy did recall something about red skies. "I'm not sure that's entirely correct," he giggled.

"I'm off on my travels again now, but if I were you I'd go back to bed."

"Sound advice, young Timmy Turner. I think I will."

"I've had the best time with you, Sir Harington."

"Likewise, Timmy. Good luck on your next adventure." He saluted Timmy and crawled back under the bush, where he promptly fell asleep.

Timmy and Mr Poops wandered back through the formal walled garden to the place beneath the wisteria where they had left the time-travelling toilet. Timmy was relieved to find it still there.

"I wonder where we'll go next?" he said to Mr Poops as he reached out to flush the lever upwards once more.

The toilet was its usual temperamental self and it took three flushes to get the water to begin to move, but soon the swirling colours returned and, once again, Timmy and Mr Poops were sucked back into the plumbing of time.

Chapter Seven

The colours stopped swirling once more and Timmy and Mr

Poops found themselves plunged into total darkness.

Although Timmy was pretty sure they had reached their

next destination, curiously he felt as though he was still

moving. It was hard to regain his bearings and he was

starting to feel quite hot and sick. He thought that maybe

he'd eaten too much at the banquet.

There was a strange smell in the air. It was not a good smell;

it reminded him of the sad day when his hamster, Mrs Fluff,

had died.

Timmy tried to focus on his surroundings; he listened

intently and was sure he could hear the sound of water

surging, like waves on the sea. That would explain the

sickness at least. Timmy was a terrible sailor – he had once

been sick when floating in his paddling pool on a rubber

ring. A sailor's life was not one that Timmy was destined for.

Listening more closely, Timmy was sure he could hear

voices. They were not happy, chatting voices, but more like

moaning, groaning and pained voices. Reaching out his hands, Timmy could feel a wooden floor beneath him. Stretching sideways he could also feel wooden walls, and, above his head, a wooden lid. He concluded that they must be in some sort of crate. A very hot crate.

Suddenly, the whole container slid to the side and a small circle of light became visible through a small hole in the box-shaped prison. Putting his eye to the hole, Timmy could now make sense of his new location. No more pristine gardens and beautiful manor houses for him – he now seemed to be on a large ship, bobbing up and down on the sea with bright sunshine overhead. The deck of the ship was lined with bodies dressed in red and blue military uniforms. Some had bandages wrapped around parts of them, while others had bloodstained faces. Timmy was still unsure where and at what point in time he was, and he wondered whether he should stay in the crate or try to get out. He was feeling very queasy now and extremely hot and thirsty.

Reaching up, Timmy pushed the lid; it was quite heavy, but it moved. He tried to stand, but his legs were weak and he fell down. The time travelling and sea sickness were clearly affecting him. Now he was really hot and sweaty and Mr Poops was panting too. Feeling panicked, Timmy was about to yell for help when he heard:

"I'll get some water, Captain."

The lid lifted, bright sunshine filled the crate and, as a tall man reached in to grab what he thought was a ceramic bottle of water, Timmy leapt out like a jack-in-the-box, swiftly followed by Mr Poops. He ran to the side of the ship and was immediately sick over the side and onto the head of a passing dolphin.

His head was spinning, his heart was pounding and he was panting like a puppy. A large hand gripped his shoulder.

"We seem to have a couple of stowaways on board, Captain," said the tall man in a strong Scottish accent.

And with that, Timmy fainted.

***

Opening his eyes once more, Timmy found that he was still

in the middle of the sea and the sun was still blazing, but

now he had a damp cloth on his pounding head, he was in

the shade and the tall man was dripping water into his

mouth from a bit of dirty old cloth. Mr Poops lay at Timmy's

side lapping up a bowl of water.

"He's awake, Captain," said the man. "You gave us quite a

shock, young man," he whispered to Timmy. "You shot out

of that crate like a rat up a drainpipe. I nearly pooped me

trousers!" Timmy would have found this very funny, had he
not been feeling so ill.

He tried to speak, but he was still feeling very weak. "Here,
drink this," said the man. "You and your little wee friend
have got yourselves dehydrated. That's a killer out here."
Timmy gratefully took the small cup and sipped some water.
He could feel himself recovering a little with every drop.
"We made you some shade using an old sail," the man went
on, "to try to cool you both down."
"Thank you," whispered Timmy and he remained still and
quiet while he slowly drank his water.

Looking around, Timmy now had a better view of his
surroundings. He was on some sort of military ship. There
were many soldiers around him and they were groaning in
agony from their terrible injuries. Many had blood-soaked,
fly-covered bandages and dressings.

'Well, that explains the repulsive smell,' thought Timmy.
The tall soldier who had helped him was walking amongst
them doing his best to calm them and give them water.

"It shouldn't take much longer," he was saying. "Just a few more hours. We should get there after the sun goes down."

Timmy wondered where they were going. He hoped it was a significant improvement on his current location.

Mr Poops had finished his water, had a little nap and was now walking up and down with a look of urgency in his eyes.

"Do you need a wee, Mr Poops?" said Timmy.

Mr Poops let out a little woof.

"I'll have to hold you over the side of the boat."

Mr Poops looked worried.

"I won't drop you, I promise," smiled Timmy and he picked up his little friend and dangled him over the side of the ship while Mr Poops did a little tinkle.

Looking mightily relieved, Mr Poops was put safely back on the deck and he and Timmy sat back down in the shade. The tall soldier walked towards them.

"You should stay seated," he said. "It's unusually hot for this time of year."

"What time of year is this?" asked Timmy.

"Oh dear, you really are poorly, son, aren't you? It's November."

"Is it?" queried Timmy. "And what year is it?"

The man looked concerned. "1854, of course."

"Oh yes, of course," agreed Timmy, nodding his head. "And just remind me again, where am I?"

"Oh, my poor wee boy. You must have been injured in the battle. Were you in the charge? The Light Brigade? Did you get caught up in the fighting? You are so young. You will be first to see the doctor."

"Owwwww!" came the groans from one of the wounded soldiers who had his leg bandaged from the knee down. "I've nearly had my leg ripped off in battle. I MUST see the doctor first."

"A horse stood on my head!" cried another soldier, whose face was covered in blood. "I should be first."

"You have all suffered terribly," said the tall man. "I've been informed by the captain that a whole team of nurses is arriving at the hospital tonight led by one Florence Nightingale. They are coming to restore order and make you all better so that you can all return home to your families to recuperate as soon as possible."

"Oh, I do like nurses," said the soldier with the bandaged leg. "If it wasn't for a nurse named Mary Seacole out on that battlefield, I would most certainly be dead. What a woman she was."

Timmy listened to all of this conversation and it was becoming clearer now exactly where he was and what had happened to the poor groaning soldiers on the stench-ridden ship.

He had read, in his history book, about the Charge of the Light Brigade during the Crimean War of 1854. It had been a disastrous venture for the British army and their allies, where they had charged the wrong way into battle, straight into the firing line of the Russian army. Hundreds of men lost their lives in that battle. He remembered the words of the poet Alfred, Lord Tennyson and realised that these men were the lucky few:

Half a league, half a league

Half a league onward,

All in the valley of Death

Rode the six hundred.

"Forward the Light Brigade!

Charge for the guns." he said:

Into the valley of Death

Rode the six hundred.

Timmy knew that these men had witnessed the utter horror

of war. Timmy also knew of the famous nurses they were

speaking of. Mary Seacole was a Jamaican-born nurse who

travelled to London and sailed to the Crimean War at her

own expense. She cared for soldiers on the battlefield and

also set up a hotel, where she would feed them delicious

food.

And, of course, he'd heard of the nursing talents of Florence

Nightingale, the lady with the lamp. He was feeling quite

excited at the prospect of meeting the woman who changed

the face of modern medicine and who never gave up on her

dreams.

For the rest of the journey, Timmy and Mr Poops rested,

taking small sips of water and having short naps. They had

been on a massive adventure already and it didn't look like

it was going to end any time soon.

As the sun started to dip below the sea, the air became

cooler and Timmy felt a little better. The ship seemed

calmer and the groans of the soldiers lessened. Looking up into the darkening sky, Timmy saw millions of beautiful stars and a magnificent full moon.

The tall soldier who had been looking after everyone came and sat down next to him.

"It's beautiful, isn't it?" he said, pointing at the sky. Timmy nodded. "Even in the most war-torn places, the sky is always beautiful. I often look at the sky and think of my wife, Margaret, and my children. It gives me great comfort to know that they are sitting under the same sky, looking at the stars and thinking of me. I tell them it won't be long before I'm home – just a few more weeks. I know they can't hear me of course, but I say it anyway." As he spoke, Timmy was sure he saw a tear roll down the soldier's face.

"I'm sure everyone on this boat is grateful that you are here," whispered Timmy. "I know I am. You have been very kind to me."

The man smiled. "I'm glad to have been of assistance," he said. "You remind me a little of my son Adrian. One day, he'll do great things and I suspect that you will too."

"I hope so," smiled Timmy. "What is your name? You have spent all day looking after me and I don't even know what your name is."

"I'm William," said the soldier. "William Hope."

"Great name – Hope," replied Timmy. "It's always good to have hope."

William smiled. "Yes, it is."

"LAND AHOY!" came a shout from the ship's captain. "All hands on deck!"

"That's my cue to get back to work," said William, standing up. "You never told me your name, young man."

"I'm Timmy Turner," said Timmy "and this is Mr Poops."

"Timmy Turner, eh. I will keep an eye out for you, my boy – great things are heading your way. I can feel it." He stood up. "I'd better get back to work, as we'll soon be at the hospital."

And, with that, William went back to his duties, whistling a tune to himself.

As the boat docked in the darkness, a wooden gangway was put in place to allow all the wounded soldiers to finally leave their vessel.

"All the walking wounded first," came the captain's instructions.

Timmy and Mr Poops were ushered off the boat with a few other soldiers who were clearly very unwell. They were met at the other end of the bridge by some military porters who were waiting to escort them to hospital.

Stepping onto dry land, Timmy felt a deep sense of relief. Although his legs still felt as if they were tottering around on the ship, his eyes were telling him that the land was solid and still. It was quite a strange sensation. Looking at Mr Poops, who was swaying a little from side to side, Timmy realised that dogs were also susceptible to a dose of sea legs.

As the last men were stretchered, moaning and crying, from the ship, and the crates of supplies were loaded onto the carts of awaiting horses, Timmy saw William Hope disembarking and joining the soldiers. William turned and saluted the captain, walked to the front of the line and shouted his orders.

"To the hospital! Quick march."

Timmy and Mr Poops began to walk slowly with their comrades through what looked like a very small, quiet town and up a very steep hill towards an old military fort.

The air was warm and very dry, the ground felt dusty underfoot and there was a wonderful sound of crickets chirping in the moonlight. It reminded Timmy briefly of a Mediterranean holiday he'd been on with his family and, all of a sudden, he felt a little homesick. He was missing his mum and dad and his brother and sister. He wondered what they were doing right now. Would they be looking for him? Of course not. They wouldn't even know he was gone because (with any luck) future Timmy was back at home, where he belonged, carrying out scientific enquiries in the bathroom. Only he and Mr Poops would ever know about this time-travelling adventure. Timmy felt reassured by this. After a few minutes, they reached a large wooden door at the old fort. Surely this wasn't the hospital, Timmy thought. William knocked loudly on the door with his large fist. It was opened by another tall soldier who spoke to William briefly, handed him some papers to sign, and then gave the orders to bring them in.

Chapter Eight

Timmy had no idea what to expect from an 1854 Turkish military hospital, but he really didn't expect the sight and smell that greeted him. In the candlelight, Timmy could make out the bodies of sick and wounded soldiers all over the floor. They were wrapped in filthy, blood-soaked sheets and they were clearly very ill indeed.

The smell was intense – the sort of smell that comes from rotting meat, but combined with the scent of disgusting toilets and the added tones of 'eau de vomit'. It was completely overwhelming; it was no wonder these people were dying at such alarming rates. Timmy felt sick to his stomach.

"This is no place for a young boy," said a familiar voice.

"Timmy Turner, you and your canine friend will be sleeping in my quarters tonight. You can have the bed; I'll take the floor." It was William Hope.

The look of relief on Timmy's face was clear to see, even in the gloom of the hospital. William put a hand on Timmy's shoulder and escorted him out the ward, along a narrow corridor and to a small room. Inside was a wooden-framed canvas bed that was covered with a couple of army-issue blankets. It had an enticing-looking soft white pillow at one end.

"You can stay here," he said, lighting a candle with a match he'd taken from his pocket.

"Thank you," said Timmy. "Thank you again. Now you have saved my life twice today."

"Don't mention it. It's my job to look after you and all the other soldiers. And I will look after you as if you were one of my own children. Now, I've just got to unload the supply crates from the carts and then I'll be back. You two make yourselves at home."

William left, closing the door behind him.

Timmy and Mr Poops settled themselves into William's room, resting their weary bodies on the bed. They were both exhausted and Timmy quickly drifted off to sleep with Mr Poops at his side. He dreamed happy dreams about his family having a big food fight at the kitchen table and Mr Poops launching himself from the top of the fridge to catch a flying sausage. It was a good dream.

A few hours later, they were awoken by a shrill voice saying: "Oh no, no, NO! This will not do. It will not do at all. Ladies, we will need to roll up our sleeves and clean and organise like we have never done before."

William, who had been snoring on the floor beside Timmy, sat up. "They're here," he whispered.

"Who's here?" replied Timmy, feeling a little scared.

"Florence what's-her-name and her team."

"Do you mean Florence Nightingale?"

"Aye, that's the one. She reckons she can sort this place out and help everyone to get better and maybe even get home to their families. I don't have much hope myself, but I suppose it's worth a try."

"But *you* are 'William Hope'," smiled Timmy. "I think you might be quite surprised at what Florence and her nurses can do."

"We'll see. We'll see," said William, lying back down. "Let's get some more shut-eye before we meet the nurses, shall we?"

Timmy placed his head on the soft pillow and dozed a little longer. He was awoken a while later by a rough tongue licking his face. Mr Poops needed to go outside.

Sitting up, Timmy noticed that William had gone. There was a stream of light coming in from a small window above the bed and Timmy looked out to see a small courtyard garden with a few fruit trees in the centre. 'Perfect,' he thought. Climbing off the bed, he put on his shoes, opened the door and tiptoed out into the corridor to try and find a way to the garden. With Mr Poops at his heels, Timmy quietly closed the door, turned right and walked along until he came to a gap in the thick stone wall.

In front of him was another large wooden door. It was slightly ajar and so Timmy pushed it open and wandered into the small garden. Mr Poops threw caution to the wind and ran to a corner. He looked mightily relieved to be relieved!

The small area was not as pretty as the beautiful formal gardens of Sir Harington's estate, but it had a certain charm to it. Surrounded on all sides by white painted walls, which were draped with grape vines and bright climbing flowers, the garden had a group of citrus trees in the centre that were full of oranges and lemons.

Timmy was hungry and he reached up to pick an orange, which he quickly peeled and devoured.

The taste was like liquid nectar. The sweet juice dripped down his chin and onto his shoes. Never had a piece of fruit tasted so good. Now he understood why his mother was always trying to get him to eat fruit at home. He'd been foolish to refuse her offers of these tasty delights. He licked the drips from his fingers one at a time.

"Enjoying your vitamins I see, young man," said a soft and gentle voice. Timmy turned around to see a young nurse standing in the doorway. She was wearing a greyish–blue floor-length dress, a pristine white pinafore and a white nurse's cap. She had a pale complexion with ruddy cheeks and dark hair.

"It's ok," she said. "Sunshine and vitamins are just what the doctor ordered. Well, not the doctor that works here; he doesn't know what he's doing, but I know it's what you need."

The young nurse walked up to Timmy and shook his hand.

"Florence Nightingale at your service," she said.

For a moment, Timmy was speechless. He was amazed that yet another spectacular historical figure was shaking his hand. He took a deep breath and managed to utter, "I'm Timmy Turner, nobody of any great importance."

"I don't believe that for one minute," said Florence. "Everyone is important. I've heard all about you, Timmy Turner. Mr Hope said that you have been through the wars... much like everyone else here. From the way you scoffed that orange, I'm guessing that you need a good, nutritious meal, so let's go and get you some breakfast."

Timmy agreed. He was starving and his tummy was rumbling. "Come on, Mr Poops," he called.

"No, no. Your little friend may not enter these walls again. No animals in here. This is a clean and hygienic space."

"But…" started Timmy, "he's my best friend."

"Be that as it may," replied Florence sympathetically, "we cannot allow animals in the hospital, no matter how adorable they are. I tell you what I'll do – I'll have my cook bring him some nice sausages and water and I'll have the handyman make him a small kennel today, I promise. It's important to care for all of my patients, furry or otherwise."

Mr Poops looked very pleased at the mention of sausages and fresh water and he sprawled out in the shade of the fruit trees to await his treats.

"Okay," said Timmy. "It's a deal."

***

Florence and Timmy went back to William's room. "Now then, Timmy Turner. I understand that you have been quite unwell?" enquired Florence. "Dizzy, sick, hot and delirious – not knowing where you were or even what year it was. Is that correct?"

"Yes," said Timmy, "but I'm feeling much better now after my sleep."

"Well, sleep is a good healer and so is cleanliness, nutritious food, clean water and fresh air. I aim to ensure that each of my patients receives all of these things. Now, hold out your hands please."

Timmy held his hands out in front of him, even though they were quite sticky from the lovely juicy orange he'd just eaten. They also had bits of dust on them from the garden, a few hairs from Mr Poops and something brown and slimy that Timmy wasn't quite sure about.

"Hmmm," said Florence, checking them front and back. "This will never do." Timmy felt a bit ashamed and he wondered what his mum would say if she saw them.

"My mother always tells me to wash my hands," he told Florence. "Especially after going to the toilet. She sings a song to me that goes like this: 'If you don't wash your hands when you go to the loo, you might get a tummy ache and have runny poo!'"

Florence gasped! "Well, I'm sure that's not in any medical book I've ever read, but it sounds like very sensible advice. I will add that song to my nursing curriculum when I return home. You should listen to your mother, Timmy Turner. She sounds like a very sensible woman. Now, your first job of the day is to have a bath and change your clothes. I will have one of my nurses show you the way, and then you must return to your room and I will see that you have some breakfast brought to you."

"That sounds good," said Timmy. "Thank you very much."

"Not at all. Now, I'd better get back to work. There is so much to do – the new beds and clean sheets are arriving this morning. If you wait here, a nurse will be along shortly." And, with that, Florence walked purposefully down the corridor. Timmy was sure he could hear her humming the handwashing song to herself.

He sat on the bed and waited. He looked out of the small window and he could see Mr Poops, who was fast asleep under the orange tree. His legs were twitching – he must have been dreaming about chasing next door's cat again.

Within a few minutes, there was a knock at the door. It opened and another young nurse in her smart uniform came in holding a clean white nightgown and a towel.

"Master Turner?" she asked.

"Yes."

"I'm nurse Evangeline. I've come to escort you to the bathroom and to give you this clean nightgown. Follow me please," she instructed.

Timmy followed Evangeline back along the corridor to a door at the far end. Opening the door, Timmy wasn't sure what to expect. Surely there wouldn't be a fully plumbed bathroom in a Turkish military fort? Peering around the door, Timmy saw half an old wooden barrel in the centre of the sparse grey stone room. Next to the barrel was a tin jug and in the corner of the room was a metal bucket. Timmy looked to nurse Evangeline for some sort of instruction.

"You can bathe in the barrel," she said, seeing the look of confusion on his face. "It's not ideal, but we are awaiting the arrival of some tin bathtubs, so we are making do. I've filled it with warm water for you and there is some soap in the jug. If you leave your dirty uniform outside the door, I will see that it is laundered and returned to your room. If you don't mind me saying, Master Turner, you have a very strange uniform; it's not one I've ever seen before in the British army."

Timmy looked at his clothes – his grey tracksuit bottoms and white, somewhat grubby, T-shirt.

"I'm in the secret service," he said quickly. "I can't really tell you much more than that. You understand, don't you?" He tapped the side of his nose with his finger.

"Oh yes, of course," she nodded. "I'll say no more about it. This is your nightgown. You can wear it while you are convalescing, and this is a clean towel for you."

Timmy took the towel and nightgown from Evangeline.

"What's the bucket for?" asked Timmy, dreading the answer.

Evangeline looked a little embarrassed. "That's the lavatory," she whispered. "You can do your business in there and just outside that door over there is a large hole in the ground where you can empty it."

Timmy noticed the second doorway, which appeared to lead out into another yard.

"Oh, I see. Thank you, Evangeline."

"Is there anything else you require, Master Turner?"

"No thank you, you have been really helpful."

"Then I will leave you to it," she said and she went.

Timmy was alone in the grey stone bathroom. He quickly made use of the bucket, following Evangeline's instructions, before undressing, dropping his clothes around the door and into the corridor and stepping into the half-barrel bath. This was, without doubt, the strangest bath he'd ever had, but also the most appreciated. He hadn't had a bath for centuries and he'd been so hot and sweaty that the warm, fresh water was a welcome relief. Being so small, Timmy found that he could sit in the barrel with his knees folded beneath his chin. He reached for the jug and the soap and felt the water run down his face as he poured it onto his hair.

The soap smelled of rosemary and lavender and little bits of both were visible in the bar. Timmy had never enjoyed a bath so much. At home, he was always reluctant to wash, but this was heavenly. He enjoyed the peace of his surroundings, the freshness of the water and the feeling of being clean at last. He soaked in the water until his fingers and toes went wrinkly, before he climbed out, dried himself, put on his nightgown and shoes and went back to William's room feeling as fresh as a daisy. As promised, his breakfast of eggs, toast and fresh water was waiting for him.

***

After breakfast, Timmy sat on the bed and looked around the room. There wasn't much to see: grey stone walls, a grey stone floor and a bright-red military uniform that was hanging on the back of the door. In the corner of the room was a wooden chair and a small writing desk that had on it a little jar of ink, a pen, some paper and a book.

For someone who had so little, William Hope was a very generous man, Timmy thought.

Just then, there was a knock at the door. It was Evangeline.

"How are you feeling after your bath, Master Turner? No dizziness or faintness I hope?"

"I feel much better," he replied.

"You certainly smell better," giggled Evangeline. Now it was Timmy's turn to feel a little embarrassed. Did he really smell that bad before? "I've come to take your breakfast tray back to the kitchen."

Timmy handed Evangeline the tray.

"Is there anything I can do to help you?" he asked.

"Everyone has been so good to me. I'd like to repay you all a little."

"You *are* feeling better, aren't you?" she smiled. "Well now, let me see. Miss Nightingale does like patients to take part in activity if they are feeling well enough, but you must rest afterwards mind."

"Absolutely," said Timmy.

"I could do with a bit of help unloading supplies from the storeroom. Do you think you could help me? There have been so many deliveries since we've arrived that everything is in a bit of a mess."

"Yes, I'm sure I can help with that," said Timmy. "Is the storeroom where the crates from the boats are kept?"

"Yes. They are full of useful supplies that we need to get this hospital shipshape and make people better."

"Okay," said Timmy, keen to find his beloved toilet once more. "Let's go!"

Evangeline led Timmy left and down the corridor and back towards the hideous ward he'd walked through yesterday when he'd arrived. Timmy waited for the putrid smell to smack him in the nostrils, but he was pleasantly surprised to sniff the wonderful aroma of soap and cleanliness instead. Peering into the ward as they passed, Timmy saw that it had been cleared of patients and a team of nurses was scrubbing the floors and walls.

"Where have all the patients gone?" Timmy asked. "Didn't they make it through the night?"

"No, no. They are safe. We moved them to a different ward while we clean this one ready for the arrival of the new beds. Those poor men were sleeping on the floor in their own filth."

"I saw that," said Timmy. "It wasn't pretty."

"Indeed," replied Evangeline. "We hope that, with clean wards, order and good food, we can help these poor men to get better and return home to their families."

"Here we are, Master Turner," said Evangeline, stopping at a wooden door. "The storeroom."

They entered yet another grey stone room. This time, it had two lines of wooden crates on the left and a whole wall of empty shelving and store cupboards on the right. There were two small windows high up on the back wall, which just allowed in enough light to see what they were doing.

"There's a lot to do, isn't there?" Timmy noted.

"Yes, there is," replied Evangeline. "My grandfather always used to tell me that the best thing to do is one thing at a time – you'd be amazed at how much you can get done."

Timmy and Evangeline started to unload the wooden crates. They contained everything from medicines, bandages and bedpans to clean bedding, pillows and fruit bowls.

Everything was carefully put away in the labelled cupboards and on the shelves. The pair worked really hard.

"A place for everything and everything in its place," said Evangeline contentedly. "One more crate to go."

Timmy looked over to a crate in the corner of the room. It was quite difficult to get to, but he was sure that's where his toilet would be.

"I'll climb over and pass you the bits from the last crate," he volunteered.

"Okay, Master Turner, but you must promise that you will rest afterwards, as we've been very busy this morning."

"I promise," he said as he started to climb.

Reaching the corner, Timmy lifted the lid on the final crate. Bingo! There was the toilet, surrounded by a few packages and ceramic bottles of water. Timmy lifted everything out and passed it to Evangeline while checking that his toilet was still in one piece. When he was sure it was, he said, "That's it, all done," and he climbed back out of the crate and over to the young nurse.

"Evangeline," he asked, "what happens to all of these crates now that they are empty?"

"Well," she replied, "in a few days, some soldiers will arrive with new supplies and they will take these old crates back to their ship where they will sail back home to be refilled.

Until then, I'm afraid they just stay here getting under my

feet!"

"I see," said Timmy, pleased he now knew how he would

get home. "Well, I suppose they are very heavy to move

around."

"Exactly, Master Turner. Now, you must rest. I will take you

back to your room and you can have a nap before lunch."

Timmy was quite surprised at how tired he felt and he

realised that he must have actually been quite poorly on the

boat. All this time travelling was taking its toll on him. He

willingly went back to his room for a sleep.

***

He awoke an hour later to the smell of yet more delicious

food: warm vegetable soup and freshly baked bread, if he

was not mistaken. Opening his eyes, William Hope slowly

came into focus.

"Are you hungry, young man?" he asked. "I've brought you

some lunch."

"Thank you," said Timmy. "Yes, I'm starving!" He sat up and took the tray of food.

"You'll be better in no time with food like this," said William. "These nurses seem to know what they are doing after all. Do you mind if I eat mine in here with you?" He put his own lunch on the small desk and sat on the wooden chair.

"Please do," said Timmy. "It's great to have company. I'm quite lonely without Mr Poops. I hope he's ok."

"He's doing just fine," laughed William. "He's got a nice new kennel out there, plenty of food and water and all the nurses love him."

Timmy peered through the window to see Mr Poops having his tummy tickled by a young nurse.

"This food is beautiful," said William, licking his lips. "It's almost as good as my wife's cooking."

"It is delicious," agreed Timmy. "How long have you been away from your family, William?"

"Six months and counting," he replied. "I miss them all every day, like every other soldier here, yourself included I'm sure. Do you have family at home?"

"Yes, I do," said Timmy. "And I miss them all terribly." He felt a little tearful thinking about home and he was certainly feeling ready to return. He hoped that the toilet was also ready to return to his bathroom.

"Well, I'm off home in a few weeks," smiled William. "I have some leave to take and then I'll be back out here as long as I am required."

"You are a brave man, William," said Timmy.

"I'm no braver than any other soldier out here. I simply follow orders and try to look after my comrades as best I can." They ate the rest of their lunch quietly, enjoying every tasty mouthful. When he had finished, William stood up.

"It's time for me to get back to work. Have you finished your lunch? I'll take your tray back to the kitchen."

"Thank you," said Timmy, "my compliments to the chef."

"Indeed," smiled William, patting his belly. "You get some more rest now Timmy, and I'll see you later." And off he went.

Timmy spent the afternoon in the courtyard with Mr Poops. They played fetch with an orange that had fallen from the tree and they snoozed on a bench in the shade. Timmy daydreamed about all of the amazing people he had met on his adventure and he marvelled at the great things people can achieve when they put their minds to it.

He thought about some of the things he'd like to achieve in his life, like being a great inventor and engineer who can design things that could improve the lives of others. Help people to solve problems, that's what he wanted to do. After a few hours, the air began to cool and Mr Poops disappeared into his new kennel, where he had a nice blanket to snuggle in.

Timmy made his way back to his room, finally feeling like his old self once more. On his way along the corridor, Timmy met Florence.

"Good evening, young man. How are you feeling?" she asked.

"I feel so much better, thank you Miss Nightingale. The care given by you and your team has been second to none."

"I'm very pleased to hear it. You certainly look much better." She checked his temperature by putting her hand on Timmy's head.

"I think we should be able to discharge you in the morning," she smiled. Florence handed him a pile of clothes. "Here is your uniform, clean and pressed back from the laundry." His clothes smelt much fresher than when he had taken them off, that was for sure.

"Thanks," said Timmy. "I think I'll keep them like this until the morning."

"Perfect," said Florence. "Now head back to your room and supper will be brought to you in about an hour. Does lamb stew and vegetables sound good to you?"

Timmy was pretty sure that he dribbled slightly as he nodded his head, and he returned to his room for another scrumptious meal and a good night's sleep.

The following morning, Timmy woke early. The sun was starting to shine through the window and onto his pillow. He looked out into the courtyard. Mr Poops was still fast asleep in his kennel.

"Another sunny day, is it?" came the voice of William, who had been asleep on the floor.

"I'm so sorry, did I wake you?" asked Timmy.

"No, no. I'm always up with the sun. It's the best time of the day," said William. "So peaceful and calm. I hear you are being discharged today. That's wonderful news."

"Yes," giggled Timmy, "you can have your bed back."

"I don't mind the floor," smiled William. "It's good for my back." He stretched and Timmy heard all of his bones click.

"It's meant to do that!" William laughed.

"I will miss this place," said Timmy.

"This dirty old place. Why?"

"Well, I might not miss the dirt, although it seems much cleaner now, but I will miss you and the kind nurses."

"We'll miss you too. But it's time for you to go home to your family now," said William.

"Yes," replied Timmy. "I hope it is."

A short time later, nurse Evangeline appeared at the door carrying two trays of porridge with honey and fresh fruit and freshly squeezed orange juice.

"A breakfast full of energy and vitamins for you both," she smiled.

Timmy took the tray from her. He'd always refused to eat porridge at home, claiming it was something that only Goldilocks and the Three Bears would eat. How wrong he was. It turns out that Timmy Turner actually loved porridge, especially when it had fresh fruit and honey in it. He ate it so fast that he gave himself hiccups.

William laughed at him. "Steady on, my boy. Anyone would think that you'd never eaten porridge before! It's a fine Scottish breakfast, isn't it?"

"It – certainly – is!" hiccupped Timmy, peering through the window at Mr Poops, who was eating yet more sausages for breakfast.

"I'd better get to work," said William. "Lots to do. More beds are arriving soon and this afternoon we set sail on another mercy mission to collect more poor soldiers from the battlefield."

Timmy felt sorry that William had to return to that awful sailing ship. That was a memory that Timmy would be very pleased to leave in 1854.

"At least you know that you are bringing them to a place where they can recover now," he said, trying to sound positive.

"Yes," agreed William. "Miss Nightingale has certainly made a big impression already. She's sending two nurses on the boat with us. I hope they have strong stomachs and good sea legs," he said as he stood up and opened the door. "I'll be back to see you before you go," he assured Timmy, and off he went to work.

Timmy got dressed in his own clothes. He was ready to go home. He picked up the pen that was on William's desk, dipped it in the ink and wrote a somewhat splodgy note to his friend, which read:

Dear William,

Thank you so much for taking care of me. If it wasn't for you, I know that I might not have survived. Your kindness and compassion have been endless and you are one of the bravest people I've ever met. I know that one day you will be rewarded for your outstanding work.

From Timmy and Mr Poops

As Timmy put down the pen, the door opened and Florence Nightingale appeared.

"Timmy Turner," she said proudly, "I think that you might be the first soldier to be successfully treated in my hospital.

I will do a few observations to make sure you are in full fitness and then we can sign your discharge papers and you are free to go."

This news made Timmy smile. Although he had loved his time here, he was more than ready for some home comforts.

Florence set about taking his temperature, checking his pulse and making him say "Arrrrr!" She checked his ears, his eyes and his breathing and threw in a couple of star jumps for good measure, before she finally said: "Perfect. Timmy, you have a clean bill of health. You can go home. We just need to fill in this paperwork."

Timmy felt a little panicked by this, as he was going to have to answer the questions convincingly if he wanted to go home. He certainly did not want to be thrown into a Turkish prison for being a suspected spy or something.

"Name?" said Florence, but she answered her own question. "Timothy Turner. Date of birth?" she went on.

Timmy had to think quickly. He needed to be at least 16 to make this convincing. He did the maths in his head. If it was now 1854, he would have needed to have been born in 1838.

"My date of birth is 19th April 1838," he said confidently.

Florence looked at him. She put her whole hand around the top of his arm as if to measure his muscles.

"Hmmm," she said. "You need to eat more, young man."

"My mother tells me that too," smiled Timmy.

"Well, you should follow her advice. She is clearly a very sensible lady. Now then, address?"

"39 Amberly Road, Great Whittingden, Kent, England."

"And, finally, what is your army number?" asked Florence. This could have been a tricky question. However, Timmy's great grandfather, who was more than a little eccentric, much like Sir Harington, loved to tell Timmy about his time in the army. His name was Peter Small, which was ironic really because he was as tall as a giant, with feet the size of canoes.

Granddad Peter, who was now 86, loved to recount the story of the day he got his army number whenever he saw Timmy. He would always say:

"My drill sergeant came to me one day, he looked me in the face and bellowed 'SMALL! I'm going to give you a number and you will NEVER forget it'. That number was 22344152."

Then he'd do a little salute, click his heels together and say, "Gunner T. Small at your service."

Timmy loved his great grandfather and they would spend hours making paper aeroplanes together and talking about life during World War Two. He was looking forward to seeing him again when he finally got home.

"My army number is 22344152," said Timmy confidently.

Florence wrote a few more notes, handed Timmy the paper and said, "Sign here," which he dutifully did.

"Timmy Turner, you are now free to go," said Florence.

"Don't forget to take your beautiful little friend, Mr Poops, with you."

"I'd never forget Mr Poops," smiled Timmy. "Thank you so much for everything you have done for me. You are an inspirational lady."

Florence blushed. "If you have a dream, Timmy Turner, it's important that you follow it."

"I have lots of dreams," he replied. "I want to be an inventor and an engineer."

"I'm sure you can be whatever you want to be," said Florence, "but by far the best thing to be is kind."

"I'll always remember that," replied Timmy.

They were suddenly interrupted. "Nurse Nightingale, there are more supplies arriving. Where do you want them?" asked a porter.

"I'll come and help you," she told him. "I'd better get on, Timmy Turner. Work to do."

"Yes," said Timmy, "there certainly is. Thank you again for looking after me."

"Any time, young man," she said as she made her way down the corridor waving goodbye. She called back, "Can you see yourself out?"

"Yes, I can. Absolutely."

Timmy went into the garden to collect Mr Poops, who seemed very excited to see him. He also seemed considerably rounder than when they had arrived.

"Have you been eating sausages again, Mr Poops?" asked Timmy as he struggled to pick up his friend.

"Woof!" replied Mr Poops and he licked Timmy's face.

Timmy laughed.

"What's so funny?" asked the familiar voice of William
Hope.

"My sausage dog has turned into an actual sausage!"
giggled Timmy.

"Oh yes, he does look well fed now, doesn't he?" laughed
William. "It's all those nurses spoiling him day and night.
Look at those big puppy eyes," swooned William, tickling Mr
Poops under the chin.

"Did you feed him sausages too, Mr Hope?" quizzed Timmy.

"Erm, yes. Yes I did!"

They both laughed.

"I'm allowed to go home now," said Timmy

"I know. That's fantastic news and it's why I came to say
goodbye."

"I will miss you," said Timmy, feeling a little tearful once
more.

"Aye, I will miss you two too. But just think, we'll both be
home where we belong very soon," smiled William. "And

you can always look up at the stars and know that we are both sitting under that same big sky."

"I will certainly do that," replied Timmy. "Thank you for everything you have done for us."

"Think nothing of it. It was my pleasure. I'd better get back to work – there's a lot to do, as always."

"Good luck," smiled Timmy sympathetically. "Come on, Mr Poops. It's time to go. Goodbye William. You are a true friend."

They saluted each other and then Timmy and Mr Poops made their way back into the hospital to find the storeroom and the time-travelling toilet.

***

Turning left and walking along the corridor, Timmy did his best to remember the way. The trouble with military forts is that everything looks the same. However, they made their way past the ward, which was now full of soldiers who were sitting in beds with fresh white sheets and plump pillows, and a little further along on the left-hand side they came to the door that had helpfully been labelled 'Storeroom'. Checking that nobody was looking, Timmy and Mr Poops sneaked inside. Like before, there wasn't much light in the storeroom – just enough to make out the crates, which Timmy climbed over with Mr Poops tucked under his arm. He worked his way to the far corner where he knew their transport awaited. Lifting the heavy wooden lid, Timmy and Mr Poops slipped into the box. Feeling around in the dark, Timmy felt the cold porcelain toilet. He reached for the flush and pushed it upwards, saying the words, "Please take us home."

For a few seconds, nothing happened. Timmy flushed two more times, and finally the familiar spinning sensation returned. The psychedelic colours swirled around as Timmy and Mr Poops shot through the plumbing of time once again.

"I really hope we make it home this time, Mr Poops," yelled Timmy. "I really miss mum and dad and Rosie and Peter and you need to go on a diet!"

Mr Poops looked a tad offended, but he too was ready for home, for his comfy dog basket and his squeaky chew toy. They swirled around for what felt like an eternity – it was, Timmy supposed, about 165 years, but time passes at it pleases when you are travelling through it. Finally, they came to an abrupt halt and the colours subsided. Timmy was afraid to look around him and kept his eyes tightly closed. He heard Mr Poops let out a little sigh of relief and then heard a loud knocking noise and a familiar voice said: "Are you alright in there, Timmy? Don't forget to wash your hands."

It was Mrs Turner. They were home.

Timmy flung open the door and gave his mum the biggest hug he'd ever given her. "I love you Mum," he said.

"I love you too, my beautiful boy. Are you ok? Why do you smell like lavender?"

"Oh, it was just an experiment I was doing in the bathroom.

It worked really well!" he replied.

"That's great. Dinner is nearly ready, so can you come down

soon? We've got sausages and mash. Your favourite, Mr

Poops!"

Mr Poops' eyes lit up. He did like sausages!

Timmy went to his room, put away his history book and

went downstairs for dinner with his family. He was home,

where he belonged, and he couldn't be happier.

He spent the rest of the holidays playing with Rosie and

Peter, taking Mr Poops for long walks to burn off some of

those sausages, and making a rocket car in the shed with his

dad. Home was definitely where his heart was. Home sweet

home.

Chapter Nine

As with all good things, the school holidays came to an end. On Sunday night, Timmy had that oh-so-familiar feeling of doom and dread. His heart was pounding and he thought that he may well be sick at any minute. His hands were shaking and he felt incredibly small and alone.

Sure, he knew he would see all of his friends in the morning, and he had missed them, but the thought of another long term with Miss Hardvile and her spiteful, evil ways was too much to bear. Timmy cried himself to sleep, though he didn't really sleep much. His dreams descended into nightmares about school where Miss Hardvile had turned into a monstrous red fire-breathing dragon. Her claws were like daggers and her teeth were truly terrifying.

"You, boy!" she shouted at Timmy. "What is six times

seven?"

Timmy could feel himself trembling from head to foot.

"Come on, you stupid boy," she bellowed. "Six times seven.

I haven't got all day. I need to get home to walk my dog."

She drummed her claws on her desk. "I'm waiting..." Timmy

gulped. "You will never get it. You are pathetic, a

daydreamer, not worthy of my classroom or my time."

Timmy was frozen in terror. Miss Hardvile moved her scaly

face closer to him and a long, sticky, forked tongue shot out of her mouth. Timmy could smell her cheesy breath as she stared deep into his eyes.

Her snake-like tongue moved closer and started to lick the sweat from his brow.

"Yesssss," hissed Miss Hardvile. "I do like to eat boys for dinner. I think you would taste very nice indeed if you were flame-grilled!" A flash of fire billowed from her nostrils and the room was full of the sound of her evil laughter.

"Now, Timmy," she continued in a very sinister tone. "This is your last chance before you become my break-time snack! What is SIX TIMES SEVEN?... Timmy?... Timmy!... TIMMY!"

Suddenly, Timmy felt a hand on his shoulder. "Timmy," said a voice. "Timmy, wake up. It's time for school."

He opened his eyes and saw his mum gently tapping his shoulder.

"Wake up sleepy head," she said. "We'll be late for school."

Timmy rolled over to find himself face to face with Mr Poops, who gave him a quick lick on the face before he hopped off the bed and trotted downstairs for his breakfast.

Timmy didn't want any breakfast – the knot in his stomach

was hurting. He had never felt so low. The thought of seeing

that awful woman moved him to tears again. Timmy didn't

want his mum to see how sad he was, so he slowly got

ready for school, wiping away his tears on his sleeves while

Mrs Turner busied herself making packed lunches and

getting Rosie and Peter ready for school and nursery. Mr

Turner had already packed up his van and gone to work.

***

Walking up to the school gates, Timmy tried to think of a

way to get through the day. He thought about his amazing

adventure and all of the wonderful people he had met on

his travels and their words filled his head. "You are a

genius!" cried Sir Harington. "You have changed all our lives,

Timmy Turner, with a simple solution," said Kha. "I'm sure

you can be whatever you want to be," Florence reminded

him.

Bravely, Timmy stepped through the gates and onto the playground, where he met his friends. And, together, they went to do battle with Miss Hardvile.

On entering the classroom, the air was immediately filled with the toxic scent of Hardvile's disgusting perfume – a revolting mix of strong acidic tones with a hint of old lady thrown in for good measure. The one good thing about it was that you always knew when Miss Hardvile was around. As each child entered the room, they were greeted by her stony face and directed to their desks, where they were told to work in silence to complete maths worksheets that she had printed from the internet. Imagination was another area in which Miss Hardvile was lacking.

After everyone was seated and they had all responded to the barks of their teacher as she called the register, she slammed down a heavy encyclopaedia on her desk. Every child in the room jumped in their seats.

"This morning, children, we will be doing a test."

The air was filled with groans.

"QUIET!" she shrieked. "This encyclopaedia here contains more information than you will ever hold in your tiny little brains. It contains facts and figures. Facts and figures are important. I know facts and figures and I am VERY important *and* I am always right. Isn't that so, children?"

"Yes, Miss Hardvile," they all chorused like reluctant robots.

"This afternoon," she went on, "we have some very important inspectors coming to visit our school to make sure that all of you children are learning and that I am good at teaching you."

'Good luck with that,' thought Timmy, along with probably every other child in the room.

"We will do a test this morning to ensure that the classroom remains neat and tidy and this afternoon we will do quadratic equations for mathematics. That should impress them. Any questions?"

Nobody dared raise a hand. "Good, then let's begin."

Miss Hardvile produced a towering pile of test papers that was almost as tall as her. Each test paper landed on the child's desk with a whopping great thud. When everyone was ready, Miss Hardvile said, "The time is nine thirty. We will work in silence. If you need help, don't raise your hand – I won't help you. If you need the toilet, tough luck, you can go at break time. Now, get on with it."

And, with that, Miss Hardvile put her feet up on her desk and began to flick through the pages of her encyclopaedia. Turning over his test paper, which required the use of two hands, Timmy felt a deep sense of relief when he saw the exam title. "Important historical figures." For once, Timmy thought that he might actually enjoy one of Miss Hardvile's tests.

He sharpened his pencil and read: "Question one: The Great Pyramid of Giza is in which country?" And then: "Write 500 words explaining how the pyramids were constructed."

Timmy breezed through this question, remembering everything he had learned from Seth and his fantastic team of workers.

Following this, Timmy answered questions on leaders from World War One and World War Two, the Wright brothers, Amelia Earhart (the first woman to fly a plane across the Atlantic) and the great Victorian inventors of the Industrial Revolution, as well as briefly touching upon the life and wives of Henry VIII. This was the most fun Timmy had ever had in Miss Hardvile's class.

The next question read: "Who invented the toilet?"

I was drinking beer with him just last week, thought Timmy, and he proceeded to write about his dear friend Sir Harington and his marvellous invention.

After a quick stop for break time and a much-needed visit to a modern toilet, Timmy returned unusually enthusiastically to his test, where the final question said: "Florence Nightingale's ideas are the foundation of modern medicine. What were her ideas?"

Timmy hummed the handwashing song to himself as he completed his answer. That was it – he was finished. He quietly put down his pencil and gazed out of the window.

Outside the school gates, Timmy noticed a large black car pull up. Two tall, suited gentlemen emerged carrying clipboards and briefcases. Timmy thought that they must be the important visitors. He watched as they walked through the playground and up to the main school entrance.

"Timmy Turner! Stop looking out of the window and get on with your work!" came the sudden shrill command from Miss Hardvile. Timmy nearly jumped out of his skin.

"Erm, I've finished Miss Hardvile," he whispered.

"What boy? Speak up."

"I've finished."

"Impossible! That test was so difficult that a little worm-brain like you should have been busy for a week. Bring it to me; I'll mark it all wrong now, and then you can go and do your corrections."

Timmy quietly got out of his chair and carried his test paper to the outstretched bony fingers of his teacher. Handing it over, he could see that she seemed to have sharpened her fingernails into points, almost like dragon claws.

"Go away, child. I'll tell you when I'm done."

Timmy returned to his desk and watched his classmates chewing the ends of their pencils trying to answer the university-level questions that were unfairly in front of them. His gaze turned to Miss Hardvile, who had her red pen in her hand and was scowling at Timmy's work. Her lips were puckered up and her cheeks were drawn in like she was sucking the most sour sweet ever invented. Her head kept shaking from side to side and Timmy could see her mouthing the words, "No, no, no!"

The more she read, the more frustrated she seemed to become. Her face was growing redder by the minute until she was almost the colour of the nightmare dragon.

"TIMMY TURNER!" boomed the voice of the dragon. "COME HERE AT ONCE!" A long spindly finger beckoned him forwards.

"What is the meaning of this nonsense?" she screamed in his face.

Timmy Turner could feel himself beginning to tremble. He tried to speak, but the words wouldn't come out.

"Well, boy?"

"I don't know what you mean, Miss Hardvile. I answered all the questions."

"Yes, you certainly have answered all the questions... and almost every single one is wrong! You idiotic child!"

Timmy could feel himself starting to cry. He knew that every answer on that test was one hundred per cent accurate.

"Look at this question," she went on with utter rage.

"Explain how the pyramids were constructed. This was a trick question, you fool. The pyramids are one of the great wonders of the world! Nobody knows how those enormous stones were taken to the pyramids and yet you have written some utter tripe about boats! BOATS, I tell you! Boats? In a desert? Really?"

"But there were boats, Miss. The workers dug canals from the river to float boats upon to carry the giant stones to the building site."

"Utter nonsense," spat Miss Hardvile. "My encyclopaedia states very clearly that this is one of the world's great mysteries." She clawed at a page in her book.

"And this question: Who invented the toilet? Everyone, but everyone knows it was Thomas Crapper. Who is this fictional nutcase you've dreamed up in that pathetic little brain of yours?"

Miss Hardvile poked Timmy in the side of the head with a sharp fingernail. Timmy turned away in case she caught him in the eye. Looking over her shoulder, he was suddenly aware of a long dark shadow appearing around the classroom door. A man stepped silently in. Miss Hardvile hadn't noticed and the rest of the class had not dared lift their eyes from their test papers.

"I have a good mind to flush you and your test down the toilet," continued Miss Hardvile, "until you learn some proper historical facts. Facts are so very important and the facts in my encyclopaedia are all the facts known to man."

"Please, Miss," Timmy tried to interrupt, but she carried on.

"Shut up, you little wretch! I honestly don't know why I waste my time trying to teach you bunch of imbeciles – you never learn anything. I'd much rather be out walking my dog than stuck in this classroom with you!"

"I beg your pardon," bellowed an even louder voice than Miss Hardvile's.

She spun around to see a very tall inspector standing at the door clutching a clipboard.

"Miss Harriet Hardvile, I presume?" questioned the inspector.

She nodded.

This was the first time Timmy and his classmates had ever seen the old dragon speechless. It was also the first time that anyone had ever discovered that she had a first name other than 'Miss'.

"Miss Hardvile, I could hear your 'feedback' of this young boy's work from the end of the corridor."

Miss Hardvile looked bemused. "But you weren't supposed to be arriving until this afternoon, when we were doing quadratic equations," she uttered in shock.

The inspector ignored her. "I can confirm that young Timmy here is absolutely correct on both these questions, and that threats to flush small children down toilets are not in any teaching manual I've ever read. I suggest you buy yourself an up-to-date computer and discard this encyclopaedia from 1985 immediately!"

Miss Hardvile looked offended and she picked up the book and hugged it close to her chest.

"Now, Miss Hardvile, as you would rather be walking your dog than wasting your time not teaching these poor children, I advise that's exactly what you do. Here is your coat and here is the door."

"But, but…" she tried to intervene.

"But nothing," said the inspector, ushering her out of the door. "You are dismissed from teaching with immediate effect. Goodbye."

And, just like that, the nightmare dragon finally left the building.

For a second, the whole class fell silent, not quite believing what had happened. Then, suddenly, the room erupted into the loudest, happiest cheers it had ever heard. "We did it! We are free!" cheered the children.

They all ran to the window to watch Miss Hardvile drive her battered old car out of the carpark for the very last time.

Timmy walked over to the inspector.

"Thank you," he said.

"You're very welcome, young man," smiled the inspector. "We can't have your enthusiasm for learning crushed by someone who knows nothing of either enthusiasm or learning now, can we? For all I know, you might be the next

world-famous inventor. You are certainly a fantastic
historian, young man."

Timmy smiled. "Thank you," he said again.

***

Harriet Hardvile never did return to teaching. Instead, she
turned her passion for walking her dog into a business.
'Walkie Talkies' was her very own dog-walking company
where she would take her canine friends for very long walks
and tell them historically incorrect facts from her
encyclopaedia. She had never been so happy and all of the
local dogs and dog owners loved her.

The children were much happier too. The following
morning, they were joined by a supply teacher, Mr Fisher.
He was a history graduate and a brilliant teacher. For one
thing, he actually liked children and valued their ideas and
opinions. He always encouraged his pupils to be the best
they could be, and he loved hearing about Timmy's latest
inventions. He was most impressed by a story Timmy wrote

for his homework one weekend, which was about his adventures with a time-travelling toilet and his faithful sidekick Mr Poops.

Mr Fisher was such a good teacher that he was offered a permanent job and he gladly accepted. He often told the children stories about how people had told him he was a no-good daydreamer, and how daydreamers are really some of the best people. "Without daydreamers," he would say, "how would we change the world? How would we learn new things? We would have no art and no music. All our buildings would be square boxes and our lives would be very dull. Please children, always be dreamers – the only thing that should limit you is your own imagination."

Timmy Turner was still a stick of a boy with scruffy brown hair, eyes like chocolate buttons and a fantastic imagination. He knew that, one day, he would be that world-famous inventor. But, for now, he was happy to just be a boy who loved school, loved learning, and happened to

have the world's first time-travelling toilet.

THE END

Can you draw a friend for Mr Poops?

A message from the author...

Thank you so much for buying a copy of this book, it really makes me smile that children (and grown-ups) are reading and enjoying my stories.

By purchasing this book, not only are you making me do a little happy dance, but you are also supporting The Play Well Trust, my non-profit organisation, which uses the power of play to support children who are seriously ill and their families. I donate 20% of profits from all sales of my books to The Play Well Trust, which enables us to support more children and families through play based activities.

To find out more about the work we do at The Play Well Trust, visit our website: www.theplaywelltrust.com or find us on Facebook, Instagram and Twitter!

And, as a big thank you, here is the link to my other website, The Do Try This at Home School, where you will find a wide range of **FREE**, creative learning activities that you can try at home as a family. Lots of fun for everyone!

www.thedotrythisathomeschool.com

Again, you can also find us on Facebook, Instagram and Twitter.

I hope you enjoyed the story, my other books are also available on Amazon and all links are on my websites.

Thank you for your support,

Sarah Vaughan

48458793R00117

Printed in Poland
by Amazon Fulfillment
Poland Sp. z o.o., Wrocław